AKELA RENAE

Published by: Purposely Created Publishing Group™
Printed in the United States of America

ISBN: 1-942-83803-4
ISBN-13: 978-1-942838-03-6

Special discounts are available on bulk quantity purchases by book clubs, associations and special interest groups. For details email: Sales@PublishYourGift.com or call (888) 949-6228.

For more information, log onto
www.PublishYourGift.com

Dedication

To the memory of my father, Gregory McDonald, Sr,
who spurred my love of reading and writing.
Thank you Daddy, I miss you, your wisdom,
your jokes and your laugh.

This book is also dedicated to my mother, Connie,
who supported me emotionally, financially and most
of all spiritually. Thanks Mom, I love you much.
Let's get ready for book two.

Table of Contents

Acknowledgements

There are so many people to thank for their help in making this book a reality. First and foremost, I have to thank God for giving me the dream. Several years ago, the airport scene of the story came to me in the form of a dream. I woke up from my slumber, pulled out my Mac and typed out all that I could remember and put it away. It wasn't until late last year that I decided to flush it out and make it a story. Dreams do come true.

Special thanks goes to TM Duncan, my editor. Trelani and I met at the last Black Writer's Conference in 2012. Our attendance at the conference was meant to be as we met several people that weekend, which have become life-long friends. Trelani, thanks for the advice, the gentle prodding and coaching throughout this process.

I also have to thank Tieshena Davis at Purposely Created Publishing Group, for making my little one the published product that you're reading today. Thanks Tie for your help, suggestions and reassurance along the way.

I cannot end without thanking my family and friends for your support, love and encouragement during this process, especially for the way you ALL asked, "how's the book going?" You'll never know how that one question would jumpstart the keystrokes on my computer when I didn't have a real answer.

Lastly, I want to thank you, the reader, for deciding to purchase my first book. I hope you enjoyed reading it as much I enjoyed writing it. Trust me, there are many more to come.

Akela Renae

• *Chapter 1* •

The commute to the doctor's office was short. To take her mind off the pending news, she flipped to Kirk Franklin's Praise on Sirius XM. The gospel music helped, but it didn't seem to calm her nerves. She said a small prayer, "Dear Lord, whatever I find out, I hope that it's in your will. Guide, direct and keep me. I love you, Lord. Please be with me. Amen."

"I guess I will have to go in and face the music," Monique said to herself as she walked into the building. Monique rubbed her eye in an attempt to keep it from twitching as she approached the receptionist. The nervous twitch started when she was in college. While she didn't have any real fears about not graduating, it was the anxiety of waiting on that final word that sent her nerves into a tailspin.

Looking around the waiting room, Monique was surprised to see there were no patients waiting this afternoon. It was crowded every time she had an appointment.

Dr. Johnson was the sole provider in this office and he decorated the waiting room himself. He had chosen a tropical oasis theme. On display were photos of sailboats and families on vacation at varying islands. Seashells were placed sporadically throughout the waiting room as part of the decor. Whenever Monique was in the waiting room, she promised herself that she would take a Caribbean vacation. Unfortunately, she never got around to it. As she stood waiting to hear how her future was going to be affected, she wished she had taken that vacation.

"Yes ma'am, how can I help you?" asked the receptionist, a stout, white woman with a grim look.

"I have an appointment with Dr. Johnson," replied Monique. She tried to sound as assured of herself as she possibly could, but felt that all her confidence was lost every time she opened her mouth.

"Name?"

"Daniels. Monique Daniels."

"Uh, are you sure you have an appointment today?" the receptionist asked, looking at her over the top of her glasses. "I don't see your name on the list," she said as she waived the list at Monique. She reminded Monique of Mrs. Garrett on *Diff'rent Strokes*, but meaner.

"Well, that's what the nurse said." Monique was getting upset now. She didn't need to deal with this woman today.

"Who did you talk to?"

"I don't know. The woman just called and asked me to come in to review my test results." Saying that aloud made Monique want to go hide in a corner and cry. She was fragile and this woman was breaking her down every time she spoke to her.

"Oh, you're a test reviewer. Uh huh, okay." She looked at Monique as if she had cooties. The women yelled to someone in the back office. "Rhonda, we got a patient here wanting to know about her results."

A test reviewer, what the hell is that?

A sista came to the window. "Are you Ms. Daniels?"

"Yes, I am," Monique said timidly. The confidence she thought she had was gone.

"I am so sorry about the confusion. I'm Rhonda, the one who called you. Please take a seat and I will be right with you." Rhonda turned to Marilyn with a look of annoyance with a raised eyebrow and her hand on her hip when she spoke to the receptionist. "Marilyn, can I see you in my office?" The two got up and walked around to the back. Monique could only hope that Rhonda was reprimanding Marilyn for her behavior. When Marilyn came back to the desk, she was clearly shaken and was as red as her hair.

Ha, ha, that's what you get.

Rhonda appeared at the door and called for her to come back. "Ms. Daniels, how are you doing today?" she asked as she escorted Monique to an office.

"A little nervous, but I'm okay."

"I have to apologize for Marilyn's behavior, she's new. We have been working with her customer service."

"Don't worry about it."

Once in Dr. Johnson's office, Rhonda said, "He will be in in a moment. Take a seat and make yourself comfortable."

"Okay, thank you."

Monique had never been in Dr. Johnson's office. Whenever she came for an appointment, she was always seen in the exam room. The same theme that was in the waiting room continued in the office. He had beautiful jars of sand and seashells of varying colors. There were also photos of his family on vacation. The nurse, Rhonda, was in all of the photos and so were children—two boys and a girl. All three kids looked just like their parents. Monique noticed the age progression in each of the photos. By the last photo, she'd guessed that the kids were roughly 16, 18 and 21. Dr. Johnson's degrees were also on display. He attended Meharry Medical College in Tennessee and completed a residency at Baylor in Texas.

Dr. Johnson appeared at the door. "Monique, how are you?" he asked as he closed the door.

Monique stood. "Hi, Dr. Johnson. I'm nervous. How are you?" The two shook hands and were seated, Dr. Johnson behind the desk and Monique across from him. Her curiosity got the best of her. It always did. "Is Rhonda your wife? I see that she is in all of your photos."

"Yes, she is. We've been married for nearly 25 years."

"She seems nice."

"I think so too." The two laughed and that calmed Monique a bit.

"Well let's get right to it, shall we?"

Monique nodded. She clasped her hands in her lap.

"Your test result for HIV is negative."

Monique let out a sigh of relief, finding out her HIV status was the one thing she was worried about. Hearing the negative result made her body fall limp. She had been carrying the anxiety in her shoulders. Tears began to form in her eyes.

Dr. Johnson continued, "However, you have chlamydia and you're pregnant."

"What?"

"You're pregnant and, judging by the timeframe of your last menstrual cycle, I am going to say you're about four weeks along."

"No." Monique hadn't had an STD since she was in college. She had gone to a band party and had a little too much Woo-Woo juice. Because no one knew what was in Woo-Woo, you weren't supposed to drink that much of it. But when it came to celebrating, those rules were thrown out. The school was partying because the football team had won against State. In celebration mode, Monique decided to go home with a football player whom she barely knew. He wanted her so she was down. A few days later, she had intense burning and pain when she urinated. She went to the health clinic on campus and they diagnosed her with gonorrhea. She vowed then that she would never again have casual sex or one-night stands.

Stunned, Monique sat there with a look on her face that said 'you're lying to me.' But he wasn't lying and as badly as she wished it was, this wasn't a dream. A tear fell from her eye and landed on her lap, affirming that this was indeed real life. She was both pregnant and infected with a disease. The tears began to fall faster and she was too embarrassed to make eye contact. She looked down at the floor as she wiped her face. If she could've snapped her fingers and disappeared, she wouldn't have even said bye.

Coming from around the desk, Dr. Johnson sat next to her. "Monique, you have options and we can take care of the disease," he said, handing her a tissue.

Finally looking up at him, she asked, "Did you just tell me that I have Chlamydia? I'm too old to be getting an STD. At 33, you would think that I would know better. And I'm pregnant? Oh, my God. What else you got to tell me, Dr. Johnson?"

"Monique, nearly three million people are diagnosed with Chlamydia every year. I'm going to write you a prescription for a one-dose antibiotic. We caught this in time before it could affect the baby." Putting his hand on her shoulder, he said, "We need to get your partner tested and treated as well."

"I don't know about that, but I will see what I can do." This wouldn't be the first time that she didn't tell her sexual partner about her diagnosis because she surely didn't bother telling the football player back in college either.

Dr. Johnson got up to write the prescription. "Get the prescription filled and take it before bed tonight. This should clear up the infection. Here is a list of prenatal vitamins that you should start taking. Wait a week before starting them. I don't want it to interfere with the antibiotic. I would like to see you in a month."

"I can't believe I'm pregnant."

"Shock is a common reaction to unplanned pregnancies. Here, this should help," he said handing her some papers. "It's a pamphlet on pregnancy that identifies some things you may start to experience. There are also a few recommendations of activities you should stop doing. Drinking alcohol is one of them."

In a daze, Monique got up from the desk. "Thank you." The two shook hands and Monique walked out of his office to the receptionist desk. After hearing the news from Dr. Johnson, Monique didn't have it in her to deal with Marilyn.

"Ms. Daniels? I am so sorry for the way that I acted this morning. I should have been more professional. I apologize," said Marilyn. "Do you need to make a follow-up appointment?"

Monique nodded her head. "I'm not sure when I'm supposed to come back. I just found out I'm pregnant."

"Congratulations. Dr. Johnson likes seeing new moms in the first month. Let's schedule your next appointment in three to four weeks." Marilyn continued talking to her, but Monique could not comprehend. Her mind was stuck on the tiny human being that was growing inside of her; following her everywhere that she went; feeding from her and depending on her for survival. It hit her that she was already a bad mother, having put her child in harm's way with the infection. The two finished scheduling the appointment and she walked to the door.

Before walking out the door, Monique had a change of heart and turned around. She had to set the receptionist straight. She walked straight up to the desk and leaned her face close to the glass. "By the way, not all pregnancies warrant a congratulations. You may want to remember that for the next patient." She left the office not caring to hear Marilyn's response.

When Monique arrived at her appointment, she was so distressed that she left her phone in her car. She had three missed calls—all from her best friend, Lena. The two had been besties for the last ten years. She called her back.

"What happened?" Lena said. "I've been calling you. What happened? Are you okay?"

"Lena..."

"Yes? Monique? Speak up and hurry up and tell me. You're scaring me."

"Lena, I'm pregnant." She left out the little detail about her having an STD.

"What? How far along are you?"

"He said I'm four weeks pregnant."

"Oh my God, congratulations, friend. That is great news. I'm going to be an auntie. Wait, who is the father?"

"I basically just cussed out the receptionist for congratulating me. So I don't feel like accepting your congratulations yet. I still can't believe it. You know what?"

"No."

"I am in no mood to go back to work today. I'm going home so I can go to bed and process this."

"Uh, sorry that I jumped to congratulate you," Lena said.

"This news has me on edge." Monique sat in the parking lot with the car in drive and her foot on the brake. She couldn't make herself move.

"I don't blame you, but shouldn't you start saving your vacation time? You never know how much time you are going to need off with the baby coming."

"Oh my God! I am having a baby!" Monique screamed. "I gotta go... I will call you later on this evening."

She hung up, knowing that she would not call Lena back. She needed to wrap her head around the fact that she was pregnant and wouldn't have the support of a man, especially the father. She barely knew him. This wasn't Monique's plan of how she wanted to start her family. She was supposed to be in a committed relationship with her husband. They both would have great careers and then mutually decide and plan to start their family. This pregnancy was messing up her plan. How was she supposed to get a man now with a baby?

Monique texted her co-worker, Craig, to let him know that she wasn't coming back to the office. He asked if she needed anything. She didn't respond to his question, but merely said that she would see him tomorrow morning. On her way home, she stopped by the pharmacy to pick up her prescription. She went through the drive-thru because she didn't want to face anyone while picking up a prescription for chlamydia. *What would the cashier think? What if I see someone that I know?*

When she got home, Monique tried to sleep for a few hours, but she kept having visions of babies. *I'm having a baby with no man in my life that this baby can call Daddy. How am I going to go to work with my swelling belly and no ring? People are going to think I'm a hoe. And I have an STD? I guess I am a hoe.*

Later on that evening, Monique's doorbell dinged. No need to look through the peephole; she already knew who it was. She opened the door to find Lena there with a teddy bear. "I thought I told you that I would call you later," she said as she hugged her friend. The two friends embraced and rubbed each other's back in a circular motion while they hugged. It was a sign of endearment that they shared since they met. Monique was never one for long hugs and had to pull away quickly. Whenever someone hugged her for too long, she felt their love. Long hugs gave her the feeling of gratefulness; and the sense of gratitude made her cry. She had been like this since she lost her father. He was killed in a tragic car accident nearly thirty years ago when an 18-wheeler ran him off the road one night. His car flipped several times and the impact killed him instantly. Monique never got a chance to say goodbye. She loved hugs, as long as they were brief. When the long ones lingered, it was time for water works. And this was one of those times.

Wiping her eyes, Monique said, "Lena, you know you can't hug me that long. I don't want to cry."

"I know, I know. But I had to come to see for myself how you were doing. Here is the baby's first toy," she said, gingerly handing her the teddy bear. "So, how are you doing?"

Monique accepted the gift but gave Lena a smirk. She didn't want a toy. She didn't even know if she wanted the baby.

The two moved to the kitchen of Monique's townhome. It was the gathering place for all of her friends when they came to visit. She had every stainless steel appliance you could think of: refrigerator, stove, dishwasher, and microwave. Her kitchen gadgets were stainless too. The cabinets in the kitchen were made of frosted glass and the countertops were marble. It wasn't necessarily a chef's kitchen, but it got the job done whenever Monique hosted dinner parties for her friends. The two were seated at the island.

Monique and Lena were complete opposites. Monique was a natural-haired sister, while Lena was forever addicted to the creamy crack. Monique was more of a vanilla latte complexion and Lena was the shade of Bit O' Honey. Monique was earthy and Lena conservative. However, in their professional lives they seemed to be wearing the other's shoes. Monique was an architect and Lena was a copywriter and working on her first novel. They both loved good music and neo-soul was their favorite. Music bonded them. The two met at a three-day jazz and neo-soul concert in Charleston, South Carolina. Lena sat a row ahead of Monique and by the second day of the concert, Monique noticed that Lena was alone.

Monique approached Lena at intermission and told her that she noticed that Lena didn't have company either. They talked a little bit during intermission and discovered they were sorors. Since they were both alone, they agreed to grab drinks after the concert. After that chance meeting, they realized how much more they had in common and that they actually lived near each other. They have remained best friends ever since.

"Thank you for the gift. I am so sorry for snapping at you earlier. I don't know how I am doing. I can't believe I am pregnant. How do I explain the fact that I am pregnant without a man?"

"Monique, trust me. You are not the first woman to get pregnant and be single, and you won't be the last."

"But this wasn't supposed to happen to *me*," she whined. "My dream was to establish myself in my career, get married, and *then* have kids. I envisioned my life to be like the Huxtables."

"Didn't we all? But I am going to tell you like my father told me, 'TV ain't real.' Yes, Cliff and Claire are the ideal, but there are a lot of women out there making it happen and raising a family all on their own. Sure, maybe it is harder, but it can be done."

"Yeah, but it wasn't supposed to happen this way. This wasn't my plan."

"Girl, none of it is our plan. You have to ask the good Lord about His plans. Have you told the father yet? Who is the father?"

"It's not who it should be, Ronnie." Monique couldn't believe she just said that, and out loud to Lena. She had been trying her best not to bring up his name. She knew that her best friend was tired of hearing about him.

Lena looked up at Monique with a look of disgust. Sensing her disapproving glare, Monique said. "Can we not talk about the child's father? I am still trying to get over Ronnie and how he walked away from our relationship—I mean our *friendship*—a year ago." She had a brief flashback of the two meeting online. She'd fallen in love with him instantly. It was his charm, his incessant sense of humor, and the way that he'd ask her how her day went. He listened and seemed to genuinely care about her. They'd been friends for two years and Monique had truly believed that they'd be together forever.

"Oh yes, Ronnie. How could I forget?" Lena said, raising her hand and then slapping it down on the table. "Monique, you've been talking about this breakup or whatever you two had going on for the last year or so."

"I know, but he broke my heart. You can't repair a heartbreak over the weekend."

"True, but you only met him once, right?

"Yes, but it was more than that. We were friends and talked several times a day. One could call it a relationship, but we never did," Monique said as she looked at the floor and mumbled. "It was the distance that kept us from seeing each other. If he and I were still friends, I would have a called him to talk about the baby."

Lena shook her head, "I think you may need to get some help. Talk to someone who can be objective and listen, especially now that you have a baby on the way. The fact that you don't want to talk about the father of the baby bothers me. As your best friend, I should know if you were sleeping with someone." She crossed her arms over her chest.

"You're right. You should know about the father of my baby. I will tell you about him in due time. So, you think I need to see a shrink or something?"

"Yes, I do. I have a referral for you if you want it. She helped me years ago."

"Really? *You* needed to see a therapist?"

"She's good. That's all I am going to say. I will write down her contact information for you. If you feel you need it, make an appointment. If not, don't worry about it. I really feel that she can help you with some of the things that you have been going through lately. Honestly, friend, you haven't been the same since you and Ronnie stopped talking and I am worried about you. You have been distant lately, and when we do talk, it's as if you are stuck on this Ronnie thing. I should have told you this months ago, but I kept hoping that you would snap out of it. I am worried that this has gone on too long."

"I don't know about seeing a shrink. Let me think about it," she said as she grabbed tissue to wipe her face. "I had no idea I had changed this much. And now, having a baby just complicates things." She sat there thinking about her future and more tears fell. "Lena, I need help. Nothing in my life is the way I planned it to be. I planned to be married by now and starting my family. Not starting my family on my own."

Lena got up to give her friend a brief hug. "Monique, things will work out. I promise, everything will be okay. Call and make an appointment with Dr. Shores. She can help you decipher things. I'm about to go and give you some time for yourself. You'll cherish all of your alone time after the baby comes. By the way, let me get all that wine you got up in here. Now that you can't drink it for the next eight to nine months."

Monique gave her the side eye. They both laughed. The laughter helped ease the turmoil that surrounded her. "Let me see if I have a wine case in here so you can take *all* of my wine home."

Lena laughed. "You do that."

Monique packed up the wine and thanked Lena for stopping by. As she walked her to the door, she promised that she would think about calling the shrink. And as it stood, she leaned more toward calling the therapist. Maybe that was what she needed. The crisis that she was currently going through was only the top layer to everything that she needed answers to. Though she originally thought she didn't want to be bothered, Monique really was thankful that Lena had come over. She needed the opportunity to talk about her new life plan. All this time, Monique thought she was doing a good job of hiding her insecurities and depression.

That night, Monique contemplated her future. *Maybe Lena was right. Maybe I can raise this baby by myself, without its father or a man in my life. Who am I kidding? I saw what my mom went through raising me alone. I can't put another child through that.*

It was during these times when life events happened she wished Ronnie hadn't called off their friendship. They could talk about anything; and it was at this time that she needed him. She sent him a text out of weakness and loneliness.

HI RONNIE, HOPE ALL IS WELL WITH YOU.

Twenty minutes had gone by and he didn't respond. *Damn, I shouldn't have sent that.* On top of feeling guilty, remorseful, shameful, and stupid, she now felt vulnerable. It was her vulnerabilities that continuously put her at this point with men; sticking her neck out in order to receive sympathy and not receiving any in return, or better yet, nothing at all. She deleted the text and Ronnie's contact information not wanting to be reminded of her weakness. Tired from the day's activities, Monique went to bed.

· *Chapter 2* ·

The next morning, as Monique got dressed for work, she checked her phone. Ronnie had not responded to her text. She tried her best to keep her mind off of her situation. Now that she was pregnant, everything she saw, touched or heard related to babies and pregnancy. On her way to work, she turned to the *Rickey Smiley Morning Show*. Today was Paternity Test Tuesday and Rickey and the crew were hyping up the couple before revealing if the guy was the father or not. The child's name was Malenciaga and her nickname was Molly. Rickey was telling all types of jokes about the name. While Monique laughed, she couldn't help but to think that she could be in the same situation.

By the time she pulled up at the office, they hadn't revealed if the guy was the father or not. Even if this could be her story, she wouldn't dare give her child a ratchet name. Period.

Monique got to work an hour early. Her moment of weakness in texting Ronnie last night was the last straw. Before closing her eyes for the night, she had decided to make an appointment with Dr. Shores. She needed to sort out her feelings and deal with her issues. She wanted to call to make her appointment before Craig, her officemate, came in. Yes, she and Craig were friends, but they were co-workers too and she didn't want anyone to know that she was seeing a therapist.

At the firm—Baker, Warner and Patterson—Craig and Monique were well-respected architects and had a good working relationship. Monique thought that it was their close office space that helped cultivate their vibe. At the conclusion of their bigger projects, the partners would come to their office to give them the 'job-well-done' speech. They were, after all, what helped make the company very successful.

Monique called Dr. Shores' office and was able to make an appointment for the following week. She would've preferred to start the healing process this week, but was grateful for what she could get. If Lena said that

Dr. Shores was worth it, then she'd wait until she could get an appointment. In the meantime, she'd just have to keep her mind occupied somehow.

"Look at the early bird getting all the worms," Craig said to her when he walked in. He was a middle-aged, very attractive man, having hazel eyes and dark hair that was beginning to gray on the sides. Monique had never dated a white man before, but should she choose to, he'd be in the category. But he was a coworker, and she didn't want her personal and professional life to mix – ever. Craig and his wife had three daughters. From Monique's perspective, their relationship had been rocky, but she never asked him about it. On more than a few occasions, she heard him arguing with his wife on the phone. If she had to guess, she'd bet that he wasn't happy in his marriage. He often had to pull double duty with the parenting. So many of Monique's friends were in the same situation that it made her think twice about marriage. But then she'd see some romantic comedy and long to be in love all over again.

"Whatever, Craig," Monique laughed. "Good Morning to you too. Hey, thanks for covering for me yesterday. Did I miss anything?"

"No, you didn't. Everything okay?" he asked.

"Yes, it will be." Monique wanted to appear confident even if she wasn't.

Monique's phone buzzed.

HEY THERE, MONIQUE. HOW ARE YOU? IT'S BEEN AWHILE.

Mason. He was right, it had been awhile. Mason and Monique had been friends for several years. They met at a mutual friend's party and had been great friends ever since. Often times, they used each other to get out of the house. Monique would call Mason if there was a new movie out that she wanted to see and Mason would do the same with her. He once asked Monique to be his date at his company's Christmas party; they had a great time at the party. Toward the end of the night, Monique thought Mason made a pass at her, but she shrugged it off as too much wine. Life and an unfortunate incident on a recent vacation had come between them and the two hadn't talked as much as they used to.

Monique: HEY THERE, MASON. I'M WELL. HOW ARE YOU?

Mason: NOW THAT I HAVE HEARD FROM YOU, I'M EXCEPTIONALLY WELL. GLAD TO HEAR YOU ARE WELL. WE HAVE TO CATCH UP SOMETIME. HAVE A GREAT DAY MONIQUE.

Monique: YES, WE SHOULD. HAVE A GREAT DAY AS WELL.

Well, that was random.

The rest of Monique's day was filled with meetings and getting a new assignment. She and Craig would be working on another project together, this time a hospital expansion which would include travel to the Midwest. While she really liked working with Craig, she hated the travel part of her job—the hassle of packing, trying to fit everything in an overhead compartment, crying kids on planes, and, worst of all, delayed flights. A delayed flight would pretty much predict the rest of the day. But it would be good for her to get away and allow her time to get out of her own head space.

"Are you ready?" Craig asked.

"Ready for what?"

"The mandatory meeting. It starts in about ten minutes."

"Oh, it completely slipped my mind. Let's go," she said as she grabbed a notebook. The two walked down to the conference room on the first floor. The company had an artistic flow. The partners had the employees design the building, which had proved to be a morale booster and gave the employees a sense of ownership in the company. There were glass sculptures throughout the building of varying shapes, sizes and colors. Monique's favorite piece was a purple cloud, at least that's what it looked like to her. The way it hung, it appeared that it was floating at eye level. The artist added so much depth that it looked as if it were in 3D. Whenever Monique passed by, she would touch the cloud for good luck. There were about twenty sculptures scattered throughout the building. The owners of the firm commissioned the pieces from two young African-American artists. They were siblings and creating buzz around Clover City.

At the meeting, Monique and Craig found out that the managing partner at the firm, Leo Wilkes, was stepping down. The company said that they would look internally for an interim managing partner until a new one could be named. As soon as it was mentioned, buzz started around the meeting in the form of whispers amongst her coworkers. As Monique looked around the conference room, some of her coworkers had questionable looks on their face, while others made no eye contact at all. She figured some would want the responsibility and would be up for the challenge and others would not.

Monique, however, was up for the challenge. She was one of three black female architects at the firm, but they were too concerned about competition to befriend her. A leadership position would be new for her, but she knew she could do the job. If she got this position, it would put her one step closer to fulfilling her career plan of becoming a partner in the firm. Whenever Monique began a new job, she identified a career path that would take her to the top in the organization. Her plan didn't always work, but most times it did. Getting this opportunity would allow her to check off one item on her career checklist.

When they returned to their office, Craig asked Monique what were her thoughts about the meeting. "I think it's an exciting opportunity for the firm," said Monique. "Sure we will miss Leo, but this would be a great time to shake things up a bit."

"Well, don't you have a positive attitude about it? Consider me the pessimist, but I want to know why Leo is stepping down. Does he know something about this firm that we don't know? With this shake up, I am little worried about my job."

"Craig, you worry too much. We will be fine. In fact, I hope I'm considered for the position."

"Monique, you don't have three girls and a wife at home to worry about. As a man, I have to be sure that I can support them financially, and I can't do that if I lose my job." At the mention of his children, Monique touched her stomach. He wasn't the only one who had to worry about that.

"Craig, how do you know Leo wasn't offered a better position in another firm? Maybe he wants to take a little time off to spend with his family. Don't jump to the negative. There could be a variety of reasons why he's stepping down."

"Maybe you're right, but I want no part of that position. You can have it. I hope you get it."

"Thanks, I do too. Enough talking, let's get started on this new assignment." They worked in the firm's division that specialized in hospital design and remodeling. Monique took pride in the fact that her work somehow could enhance the life of patients all across the United States. Their assignments often lasted a year or more – from start to finish. She loved her job, and it definitely kept her busy. Designing buildings from the ground up was a true passion of hers. Once a project was complete, she loved strolling through it and thinking, *Hey, I did that.*

Monique and Craig's office had a wall of windows and two drawing boards. They each had a desk in opposite corners of the office. Some people didn't like sharing office space, but Monique and Craig did. Many at Baker, Warner and Patterson were jealous of their working relationship because their output received so much positive attention from the managing partners.

Later that afternoon Monique received a call from Dr. Shores' office. There had been a cancelation that opened a slot for her. She decided to take the appointment so that she could start talking out her feelings and working toward a resolution in her life. She wrapped up her day early that afternoon and left the office for her appointment. *I am actually about to start seeing a therapist. Is my life that messed up that it has come to this?*

• *Chapter 3* •

Monique was so uncomfortable sitting in the waiting room that she couldn't stop her eye from twitching. *You've made it this far.* The waiting room was decorated in warms colors. The couches were a cross between salmon and coral and stood out against the hardwood floors and chocolate painted walls. Even though Dr. Shores' office was trendy, it was the colors that seemed to relax Monique. In fact, Monique had even matched the office with the coral sheath dress she wore. Warm color tones like peach, orange and coral were *her* colors. At least that is what people told her all her life when she wore them. They gave her the feeling of calm and serenity, and she liked the compliments she received when she wore them. A woman walked into the waiting room and softly called her last name.

"Daniels?" The woman was wearing a beautiful deep blue dress with long sheer sleeves. *This is Dr. Shores? She's attractive.* She looked very much like the pictures on the web. Monique had briefly researched Dr. Shores before making the appointment and found that she was very beautiful and curvy. Dr. Shores was very light-skinned and had beautiful braids like Melissa Harris-Perry on MSNBC. Today her hair was pulled back in a coifed bun.

"Daniels?" she restated, looking directly at Monique.

"Yes, I'm here," Monique said as she stood and gathered her things. She inferred that it must have been a two-person office as Dr. Shores escorted her back to the office instead of a medical assistant.

"Welcome, come on back to my office. May I call you Monique?"

"Yes, please do."

"Please, make yourself comfortable. Have a seat," she said as she gestured for Monique to sit on the couch opposite her. "What brings you in today?"

"A friend of mine suggested that I come see you. I am at a crossroads in my life and I need help working through my feelings, my issues, my... *everything*. I am at a point where I know I need to move on, but I can't seem to get past the point of heartbreak."

Looking at Monique over the top of her glasses, Dr. Shores said, "I understand. Continue."

Monique stared at Dr. Shores as if she was in a trance. She was mesmerized by how Black women in professional roles seemed to have their lives together. Dr. Shores, a psychiatrist, appeared to be in the prime of her life. From Monique's Google search, Dr. Shores was somewhat of a socialite. She was involved with various charities and did countless volunteer work. Comparing her life to that of Dr. Shores', Monique felt that her life was lacking. Sure, she did community service twice a year during the holidays at the Food Bank, but she always felt like she didn't stand out enough. Whenever she compared herself to others, she never felt that she measured up. She wanted to be a woman that young girls could look up to.

"Are you comfortable?" Dr. Shores asked. "Would you prefer to lie back on the chaise over there?" Dr. Shores pointed to a chocolate, leather, gold-buttoned tufted chaise near the window of her rather large office. They were seated in an area of the office that had two beige couches and a coffee table. On the coffee table was an ornate object that took up most of the space. It was made of brass and had what looked to Monique like an elephant trunk with its tusks sticking out on the sides. A lion's head was on the opposite side, while a tree that was bearing fruit was on another side. On the last side of the four-sided object was the ear of a monkey. Monique had never seen anything like it before. She didn't think it was artistic, but it was definitely something to look at. Dr. Shores asked her, "What do you think of the piece?"

"I don't know what to think. What is it?"

"It's whatever you want it to be. I was traveling overseas and I saw it in an antique store. I don't know what it is either, but I had to have it. A former patient told me that he guessed it to be something that you could tell your hope and fears to. He said that the monkey will listen to all your problems while the lion helps you face them head-on; the elephant will sing your praises once you've accomplished your goal and the tree is bearing fruit, proving that you will get through the hard times and end up with something good to show for it. Monique was captivated by the piece. The patient's description made perfect sense. She stared at it while trying to figure out what country the piece was native too.

"Monique?"

"Yes," Monique looked up with a surprised look.

"Would you like to sit on the chaise? Dr. Shores asked again.

"Oh, I am sorry. I was drawn in to the piece." Monique got up and walked over to the chaise. She hadn't noticed much of the office when she initially walked in. Her office was similar to the waiting room, decorated in soothing corals, chocolates, and beiges. Monique sat on the chaise, and lay back. *Ah, this is much better.* It offered her the ability to talk without looking directly at Dr. Shores.

"What seems to be the cause of your crossroads?" Dr. Shores asked.

"I'm not sure where to start. I was involved with this guy and shortly afterwards, all hell broke loose in my life."

"Give me some background information on the relationship."

Monique began to tell her story. She looked up at the ceiling as if it were a source of validation. "I fell deeply in love with a man that I met on the internet. Of the two and half years that Ronnie and I were friends, we only met face-to-face *once*." She looked over at Dr. Shores for the expected eyebrow jump. Seeing none, she continued. "And, out of the blue, he called it off. He never wanted to make our friendship a relationship, so I am really not sure *what* he called off exactly. But he did it completely out of the blue. I still have his texts stored in my phone." She pulled out her cell phone and thumbed over to the text messages. Dr. Shores scribbled notes on her notepad. "About a year ago, on a Sunday morning at that, I received a text from him." Monique commenced to reading the exchange.

Ronnie: I CAN'T DO THIS ANYMORE. THIS JUST ISN'T FOR ME.

"Taken aback by the text, I replied by asking him what it was that he couldn't do anymore."

Ronnie: I CAN'T DO THIS RELATIONSHIP ANYMORE.

Me: WHAT RELATIONSHIP? YOU NEVER WANTED TO MAKE A COMMITMENT TO ME, RIGHT? SO, YOU DON'T WANT MY FRIENDSHIP ANYMORE?

Ronnie: NO, I DON'T. THE LONG DISTANCE IS TOO MUCH FOR ME.

Monique put the phone down. She looked over at Dr. Shores. "I was dumbfounded. I responded in the best...passive aggressive way that I knew how."

Me: I WISH YOU THE BEST.

"I didn't go to church that day, but I knew that I should have. I couldn't get over the fact that he did that to me. I had sacrificed so much for that 'friend' of mine. And he ends it in a text message?"

"Monique, what was your relationship like with this man?"

"I loved him. And the thing is, I loved him and only saw him one time. Through the phone, we developed a real relationship. When the only communication that you have is via the phone, it causes you to rely on conversation and ultimately it was through his conversation that I came to trust him. I was hesitant at first, but I went all in. I could see myself being his wife."

Dr. Shores looked up from her notes and focused her attention on Monique.

"That day, I began writing my thoughts and feelings down in my journal," Monique said.

"Choosing to journal was an excellent decision. It's a good exercise to incorporate into your daily living, allowing you the opportunity to pen all of your thoughts, frustrations and happy moments."

"Happy moments? I only write about the negative things that I feel and experience. Writing helps me deal with the frustrations in my life."

"Yes, the happy moments, too. They are important when you go back and reflect. Reflecting on your past entries gives you the opportunity to see your growth. I suggest doing so every couple of months," said Dr. Shores.

"Never really thought about that," Monique said. "If I were to be honest with myself, I knew something was going on. I could sense his distance over the last couple of weeks. On a few occasions, I even asked him if anything was going on, but he always said 'nothing.' All of a sudden, my *friend* says that he doesn't want to be my friend anymore." Wiping her tears, Monique continued, "A year later, and it still hurts. He was my best friend. How could he up and just decide that he was done? I loved that man. His breaking up with me snapped my heart in two pieces. I don't know why I allowed myself to get to that point again."

"When you say 'again' are you referring to Ronnie?" Dr. Shores asked.

Monique nodded. "Yes. He had a disappearing act shortly after we first met."

"Explain what you mean by a 'disappearing act'?"

"Well, as I mentioned earlier, I allowed myself to fall deep into Ronnie pretty quickly. I admitted to him that I was scared of the potential of our relationship because we became so accustomed to each other so fast. He admitted the same. We talked nearly every day, several times a day, for hours. Six months into our friendship, he disappeared."

"How exactly did he disappear?"

"Dr. Shores, he stopped all contact. I called him, sent him a few text messages and I received no response. So I deleted him from my phone and my life. I moved on."

"Did that work for you?"

"I really just wanted to take my mind off the situation, so I did a few home improvement projects and I threw myself into my work."

"So you never really moved on. You just focused your attention elsewhere?"

"Well, if you have to put it like that, then yes. I channeled my energy and attention into other things."

"From what I gather, it appears that you aren't exactly over his *disappearing act*. Am I correct?"

"Probably not," Monique replied, sounding defeated.

"You never really dealt with the hurt. Tell me, how did he reappear?"

"Well, about three months without contact, he texted me in the middle of the night. I responded to his text and he called me. I got hot, not sexually but physically. I started sweating because I thought he was reaching out because of what I had done. As it turns out, he actually never found out about it. Or at least he never brought it up to me."

"What did you do?"

"I flew out to Atlanta, rented a hotel and a car and I drove to his house. I watched his house for two days. On my last night there, I slit two of his tires. I flew back to Clover the next morning and never told anyone. After all of that hurt and anger, I still accepted him and his friendship."

"Monique, I also noticed that when you talked about your heart, you mentioned it in past tense. You said your heart *had* been snapped in two. Why?"

"You're right. I used past tense because I am doing my best to talk about my feelings in the past. It's my way of moving on, but honestly, I don't think I will ever get over him. I felt a connection to him that I have never felt for anyone. I was very comfortable with him, and could talk to him about anything—marriage, kids, religion, family, sex, and everything else under the sun. Because we only communicated over the phone, we got to know each other more intimately than face to face. He laughed at my jokes, and I his. Things were lighthearted and fun between us. I felt like we were made for each other. I didn't think I would find anyone better than Ronnie. He was the gold standard in my book. He met all of my needs, mentally and emotionally. The physical wasn't there because of the distance, but I was filled in every other way. In hindsight, I should've known it was too good to be true because whenever I talked to him about making our friendship a relationship, he backed down or changed the subject. I just took it for what it was. In my mind, I rationalized that he was afraid of the possibilities of becoming one with me and shied away from that.

As if that wasn't enough, yesterday I found out that I am four weeks pregnant. I'm 33, pregnant, have an STD, and I'm stuck on stupid over someone that dumped me over a year ago. I can't move past my relationship-slash-friendship to accept this precious gift."

"How do you feel about the pregnancy?"

"Honestly, I don't know. I guess I need to get my thoughts and my priorities in order." Monique looked over to see Dr. Shores writing more notes on her notepad. She wondered what she had said that had triggered her to write. Furthermore, she wondered what was being written. Would she ever get a chance to see it? After all, the notes had everything to do with her.

"Are you and the father in a relationship?" Dr. Shores asked.

"No. I'm not ready to discuss the father or the circumstances surrounding how I got pregnant; perhaps during our next session. I don't know how I can bring a little one into this world as a single mom. I have no man and no one for this child to call Dad."

"Is it important for you to be in a relationship?"

"Who wants to be alone?" Monique asked with a smirk.

"Are you afraid of raising the child alone?"

"Afraid? No, I'm not afraid. I just don't want to do it alone. A man would help the situation a lot."

"Have there been other disappearing acts in your life, Monique?"

Monique looked up at the ceiling again. She didn't think they would get this deep on her first visit. "Yes. My dad left when I was six. Actually, he didn't really leave—he died. It was my step-dad that left. He met another woman and left my mom and me." Monique's stepfather left when she was thirteen. It was a day that she would never forget. She was in her room when she overheard her mom crying and pleading with her stepfather. She ran to their room to see what was going on. What she saw changed her life. Her stepfather was packing his bags and her mother was on her knees begging him to stay. He acted as if he didn't see or hear her pleas. Her mother was crying and pulling on him and he ignored her as if she wasn't there. Monique didn't want to be caught peeking at them, so she went to her room and cried. Things were never the same in their house.

"Monique?"

"Sorry, I got a little lost in my thoughts. I would have to say that several men have disappeared from my life—both romantic and otherwise."

Dr. Shores spoke up. "Then we should start there. Let's explore your romantic relationships."

Monique got ready to speak but stopped short of responding to Dr. Shores. She hadn't realized it before now, but several people had disappeared from her life. "The second disappearance happened when I was in high school. As I look back at it now, it was puppy love. But at the time I thought it was *real* love." She chuckled and shook her head. "He was a very smart guy, and I was attracted to his style. He was so cool and dressed like a prep boy. You know: Dockers, plaids and vests. No one ever knocked him for his style; they accepted him as he was. He was friends with everyone at school, and some even tried to copy his style. My first. If you would have asked me back then, I would've told you that Benjamin James was going to be my husband. At the age of fifteen, I found out I was pregnant. I was so happy to share the news with him, to tell him that we were going to be parents. What did I know? Apparently nothing because once I told him, he turned into a monster. He told me that it wasn't his, knowing that he was my first and only."

Monique looked at Dr. Shores. "I lost the baby and BJ was excited at the loss. I wanted my baby and I wanted BJ. I found out I wasn't the only one that wanted him. Shortly after I lost the baby, he got my best friend pregnant. Needless to say, she and I were no longer friends. I lost the baby, I lost BJ, and I lost my best friend. That's real hurt. I had no one to talk to about the situation. I tried to talk to my mom about my feelings, but she was so upset with her own grief over my stepdad leaving, and me being pregnant at fifteen, that she couldn't deal. She was completely cut off from me. Every night, she would sit in front of the television and eat. She didn't talk much. If I tried to talk to her, she told me that I was disturbing her 'TV time.' She gained sixty pounds in the process and was *no* help. Physically she was there, but not emotionally."

"So your mom disappeared on you, too?" Dr. Shores asked.

"Yeah, I guess she did. She eventually came back though. When I came home for Christmas after my first year away at college, she'd snapped out of it. She had lost thirty-five pounds and had a new man in her life. I was happy to have my mom back."

"Would you say that your mom based her happiness on being with a man?"

Monique sat up in the chaise and looked at Dr. Shores. "That's harsh, Dr. Shores. That's my mama you're talking about. I would never say that about my mother."

"Sorry if I offended you, it was not my intent. But to what do you attribute to her snapping out of the state of mind she was in?"

"I don't know," she said as she folded her arms and sat back on the chaise. Monique contemplated Dr. Shores' question. "Mama was happy whenever a man was around. I can't think of a time when she was happy and a man was not around. I guess you're right, she was the happiest when she had a man."

"How do you think that affected you?" Dr. Shores asked.

Arms still folded, Monique shrugged her shoulders. She knew she was being a brat, but she didn't like being bested by anyone.

"Do you think you have been living in the same state of mind, considering your difficulty in getting over Ronnie?

"I never thought of it like that. This shit sucks. So are you telling me that I am messed up because of my mom?"

"I am saying that in watching your mother go through the loss of a relationship and only being happy when she was in a relationship may have affected your view of happiness, and how to be alone and still find happiness. Throughout your life, when have you been most happy, Monique?"

She uncrossed her arms, "I guess, like my mom, I equate being happy to being with a man. So now that I don't have one, how do I become happy without having one?"

"Well, it starts with changing your outlook. You just asked how to be happy without having a man. Consider why 'having a man' equals happiness. What's wrong with being happy with Monique Daniels just the way she is with no other relationship attachments?

"What? I mean I'm happy, but not Cosby show, Cliff and Claire happy."

Dr. Shores asked, "What does happiness mean to you?"

Monique stopped to think about an answer, but couldn't come up with one. She, like her mother, was happiest when there was a man in her life, whether it was a relationship or someone that she was casually dating. But she could not define what it meant to be happy. Clearing her throat to respond, she simply stated, "I can't answer that right now. I hope that in time I'll be able to answer these questions."

"I am here to help you get there. Next week, let's explore the reason why you let Ronnie come back into your life after he disappeared the first time."

"An hour is up already? I was just getting started. We can discuss it, but I have no idea why I allowed him to come back into my life."

"Well, let me give you some homework. Until your next appointment, I want you to think about why it was important for you to become Ronnie's friend again."

"Really? You want me to go back to that place?"

"Yes, it will be good for you to revisit the scene. The receptionist, Courtney, will set up your next appointment."

Both women got up and shook hands. "Thank you for your insight. I must say I am a little perplexed. I can't see it right now, but maybe everything will come together."

Dr. Shores smiled and pointed to a glass plaque on the wall and read it, "In this office, we revisit the past. However, it is only a visit; we don't stay there. When you leave this office, you live today and prepare for tomorrow. The past stays in this office." The plaque had her signature on it. "We will work on this together," Dr. Shores said as she opened the door for Monique.

Didn't she just tell me to try to figure out the past over the course of the week? The past obviously doesn't stay in her office.

Monique turned to walk out of her therapist's office and made her follow-up appointment for the next week. Walking to the car, she again wondered how her life had resorted to this. How did she get to the point of needing therapy? She was a 33-year-old successful architect. A number of women would kill to be her—until they discovered what a failure she really was. Nurturing an unborn, already un-fathered child, treating a sexually transmitted disease, and still trying to cope the loss of a man who not only refused a relationship with her, but a friendship as well. *My life has got to get better than this. Hopefully therapy helps. If not, then things could be much worse than it is now.*

• *Chapter 4* •

Monique walked up to the tapas restaurant and asked for a table outside. The weather was nice, the sun was shining and there was a nice breeze. This was one of Monique's favorite restaurants and it was very popular. They had a limited menu that changed every three weeks to feature seasonal appetizers.

Settling in, Monique watched people as they passed. She was glad that Lena wasn't there at the moment. She needed the time to clear her head and make sense of what transpired during her therapy appointment. The waiter had come, brought water and bread to the table, and was gone before she had realized it. She was too busy watching a woman share an ice cream cone with her dog. *Nasty!* Her phone rang. Thinking it was Lena, Monique answered the phone without looking at it.

"Hello?"

"Monique? It's Mason."

Twice in one day?

"How are you?" Monique asked.

"I'm doing well, now. How are you?"

"Good. Waiting on Lena to join me for dinner," she said as she fingered her hair.

"Too bad I can't join you," Mason said.

"Huh?"

"It's nothing. Do you want to get lunch next week? It's been a long time since we hung out. We need to catch up."

"Sure. Just hit me up next week and we can make plans."

"How about we make those plans now?" he asked.

"Sure, Mason. How about next Thursday at Charlie's Place?"

"Perfect! I look forward to it."

"Okay, sounds good."

"Enjoy the rest of the week, Monique. Bye."

"Bye, Mason."

Monique wondered what the phone call from Mason was all about. She sucked her teeth at his comment, 'I wish I could join you.' She remembered that he was a good listener and thought it would be good to connect and get out of the house for a change.

Lena walked up and joined Monique at the table. "Earth to Monique."

"Sorry, girl. I was too busy people watching."

Lena smiled. "Let's order some drinks. For you, virgin; for me, adult."

"Whatever," Monique smirked.

They ordered their drinks and a few appetizers to share.

"Girl," Monique said, "guess who just called me and invited me out to lunch."

"Was it that fine Mason?"

"How did you know?"

"He's been asking me about you since we got back from the Dominican Republic."

"Oh," Monique responded and looked away at a couple sitting on a bench talking and holding hands.

"What was that look for?"

"Nothing," she snapped as she picked up her water.

"Monique, I know you're keeping something from me. I do believe something happened in the Dominican between you and Mason. Spill it!"

"No, nothing really happened. We took a walk on the beach."

"If you say so. Well, he's been asking about you ever since we got back. I have been trying to get him to spill the beans about why he's interested in you, but he will not tell me anything."

"Wait, interested in me? Where is that coming from?" Monique asked as a smile began to form on her face. *I don't believe it.*

"I've said too much already."

"Now *you* spill it!"

"Okay, okay, he asked me what you've been up to these days. I suggested that he call you. He, in turn, asked whatever happened with you and Ronnie. I told him that you and Ronnie were old news. He said that was all he needed to know. I'm the one that inferred that he's interested. I probably shouldn't have said anything. I asked him why he was asking, his simple reply was 'no reason,' so I left it at that. I hadn't even planned to tell you this much. I was just going to sit back and let nature take its course."

The waiter brought their order, sat it down quietly and left their table without really being noticed.

"You weren't going to tell me?" Monique asked with a puzzled look.

"No, because what would you have thought had I mentioned it and he never approached you? You would have been expecting it, and there is nothing better than a surprise."

"I guess you're right. We're supposed to have lunch on Thursday. But now I think I would rather hang out after work. I've spent the last couple of months cooped up in the house and it's time to get out."

"So a nice intimate dinner?" Lena asked with a smirk. "Sounds like a date to me."

"No ma'am, this is not a date. We are friends and *only* friends. We are two friends that decided to get together and catch up."

"If you say so," Lena said as she took a sip of her drink with her pinky and eyebrow raised.

"Matter of fact, let me text Mason now and change our lunch to dinner."

"You better jump on that, Monique. A brother that fine will be caught up soon."

"Lena, Mason always has a girl. But like you said, he is fine and let's not forget that he has a great job."

"It's the dimples that get me," Lena said, fanning her face with her hand.

"Don't forget his body," Monique said, sipping her cranberry juice. "You know I have never thought of him in the romantic sense."

"I don't know why not. That brother has it going on and you two have always been great friends," Lena commented.

Trying to suppress a smile, Monique shushed her friend so she could concentrate on her text:

MASON, CAN WE CHANGE TO DINNER ON THURSDAY? DOES 5:30PM WORK FOR YOU? WE CAN STILL MEET AT CHARLIE'S PLACE.

Her phone buzzed.

Mason: WHATEVER YOU WANT WILL WORK FOR ME. I LOOK FORWARD TO SEEING YOU.

"That is weird. Girl, read this text. Does it sound like he's flirting?" Monique asked as she passed her phone to her friend.

"Well I don't know how a text 'sounds,' but no, I don't read that he is flirting. I read that he is being a gentleman, which is something you need in your life. And that's all I am saying about that."

Monique snatched her phone from Lena and the two laughed. Monique filled Lena in about the appointment. She told her she was nervous at the start of the session, but once she started talking, she was at ease. "Dr. Shores has already unlocked some things that I didn't realize I was holding onto. I am still very much upset on how abruptly Ronnie ended things, even though it was a year ago. I think I am still in love with him and a little obsessed with the loss of the relationship. I find myself virtually stalking him and his family."

Lena didn't comment.

"I don't know why I allowed Ronnie to come back into my life," Monique continued, "or why I thought it was important for him to be in my life. I accepted him with open arms. I felt like I backed down and let him come back without any reservations. I gave him free reign in my life when I could have avoided this whole thing."

"Let me stop you there, Monique. You don't need to blame yourself. He led you into this relationship."

Monique bit her lip in an attempt to keep the tears from forming while listening to Lena's direct and compassionate speech. She listened intently and she knew that her best friend was telling her was the truth. It would have been the same advice that she would've given another friend if she were in Monique's position.

Lena continued, "Yes, there were red flags, but I am sure it was his personality that drew you in. Everyone experiences a few red flags in their life. However, we women tend to see those flags as anything but warnings. You can't place all of that blame on yourself. I won't allow you to do that. Not here, not ever. I've said my piece; now you can continue."

"Thanks for saying that. I needed to hear it. Deep down, I know it, but sometimes a person just needs to hear it. Now, I have a homework assignment to figure out why I let him come back into my life and become friends with him after he disappeared like Houdini. Maybe it was more out of loneliness, who knows. I will figure it out before next week. Dr. Shores has me thinking about the past and how seeing my mother pine after guys may have played a part in me allowing Ronnie to come back.

Getting a disapproving silence made Monique change the subject. "I am getting to a point where I am tired of talking about him and the subject of our...whatever it was called. I am tired of thinking about it. I am tired of feeling down in the dumps. I am ready to move on to new things."

"Like Mason?" Lena asked clasping her hands.

"Uh, no ma'am." The two women continued talking and catching up at the bistro. After they paid the bill, they walked the promenade arm-in-arm for a little shopping. Monique needed to be amongst the living. She hated being at her townhome alone. Being out, enjoying the beautiful day and having a social life was good for her.

When they arrived at a boutique, Monique tried on a few summer sheath dresses. Much to her surprise, the dresses were ill-fitting. They were tight around her boobs and her hips. She had already begun gaining weight. Monique quickly put the dresses back and moved on to shoes. They should surely fit. She tried on a pair of cute sandals. As she wandered throughout the store, she thought about all that she divulged to Dr. Shores. While it was an emotional day for her, she seemed to feel a little better. Talking about everything helped. It was evident that she had things that she had pushed down that she didn't realize were there. Walking around the store in the sandals, she realized that she wasn't in the mood to shop, but time with her best friend was always priceless.

Lena came out with three pieces: a white romper, a blue and white color block maxi, and a sexy red jumpsuit. "Okay, I am only buying two. Which ones do you like best?"

"The blue and white dress and the red jumpsuit."

"I was thinking the same. Thanks. Where are the dresses you tried on?"

Monique looked down at her stomach again. "They didn't work out. I'm on to shoes now."

While Lena paid for her dresses, her phone rung. She looked at it and sent it to voicemail. Monique asked, "Who was that?"

"No one," Lena said with the roll of her eye. She offered no other explanation. Monique just looked at her. Now there was an awkward silence between them.

Monique noticed that was the third time that had happened since they had been together. She paid for the sandals and followed Lena out of the store. "Well, I am going to head home. Are you sure that you're okay?" Lena told her that everything was fine. She hugged her friend and left.

Throughout the week, Monique worked on her homework assignment and thought about her predicament. Her life was so full of her own drama that she didn't know how she could have time for a baby. She had to answer the question of why she thought it was important to have Ronnie in her life. Other than talking on the phone with him, what could she have gained from him being in her life? Perhaps it's because she didn't want to be alone and he was familiar. Although they lived in different parts of the country, she was still physically alone, but she had someone that she connected to mentally.

Chapter 5

Today was a day for revisiting the past. Monique was back in Dr. Shores' office.

"Hi, Monique," Dr. Shores said. "How are you doing today?"

"You know, I was a little depressed last night thinking about my life and how I ended up here."

"What do you mean by 'here'?" Dr. Shores asked.

"I mean my predicament. I know you asked me about being happy with Monique Daniels, but I don't know what that means yet."

"Okay, that will take some time. Did you complete your homework Monique?"

"I think so. Last night, I reflected on why I thought it was important for Ronnie to be in my life and my friend after he left the first time. I went through my old journals to understand my mental state during that time."

"That was a good idea. How did the exercise work out for you?"

"Did you hear me say that I was depressed yesterday? Thinking about the baby, not being with the father, and thinking about how Ronnie just cut me off left me a little empty. "Before I left last week, you said that the past stays in this office, and I really challenge that thought. With the homework assignment, I had to go back to the past to truly understand why I thought it was important for him to be a part of my life. I am ready to move on, especially now that I am bringing another life into the world. I have to be the mother that my child can look up to. Last week when I was having dinner with my best friend, I told her that I am getting tired of talking about Ronnie. I am tired of this depressed state of mind. But I don't know how to move on."

"We can certainly explore that. I would tell you that coming to the conclusion that you're ready to move on is a step in the positive direction. So tell me, what did you learn about yourself during your reflection time?"

"Can I read one of my journal entries to you? Maybe this will help to set the scene."

"By all means," she said, gesturing for her to begin.

Monique opened her journal and began reading, "November 21, 2011. I am so angry right now. However, friends and family tell me I should be relieved. At 30 years old, there is nothing about getting older and being alone that says you should be relieved. Recently, about six months ago to be exact, I met a really nice guy on a dating website. It's not the most conventional way to meet someone, but these days, everyone else is doing it so I gave it a try. Unfortunately, I fell in love with this man. Yeah, I said it – love. Is it truly possible to love someone that you have never met? Perhaps that is something that a mother and father experience before meeting their unborn child. But that is totally different from my situation. He quickly became my drug and I was addicted. I had to talk to him morning, noon and night. I fell hard, fast and in love with this guy in a six-month timeframe.

So why do I sit here, angry? If I truly had to answer that, I would say that I am angry at myself. I am angry for allowing myself to fall so hard, so fast. We are now heading into a two-week 'break' that I did not initiate.

The problem is, I don't know if this is really a break, or if our brief affair is officially over. I certainly hope it isn't over, but what am I left with when the other person in this relationship will not respond to my two calls or five text messages? Why am I calling this a break? For all I know, it could very well be over. Sad thing is that I envisioned this person being my husband. And as of two weeks ago, I am left with nothing. I don't even know what happened. I now know how easy it is for some women to go psycho over a guy. No, I won't go psycho, but I certainly understand. I didn't even cry this hard when my ex-boyfriend and I broke up, and that guy was actually my boyfriend!" Monique closed her journal and looked up at Dr. Shores.

"Monique, thank you for sharing that with me. How does it make you feel to read that out loud and hear it?"

"I was so stupid and vulnerable. I blame myself for this. Reading that, I see just how weak I became. I was also very hurt and lonely. I felt as though I had been rejected by someone that I had grown very close to in a short time. I never shared this journal entry with him. However, when we became friends again, I did tell him that disappearing the way he did hurt worse than my break up with my ex. And he knew how bad that affected me."

Dr. Shores asked, "So Monique, why do you think you let him back into your life?"

"Reliving this particular moment of my life felt like I had lost a best friend. At that time, I would do anything to get that closeness back. So once he came back to me, I welcomed him. I was guarded because I wanted to protect my heart. But I still longed for his friendship. I can't answer the question of why I would want to be friends with someone that had broken my heart, but I did. There's that weakness again and me not speaking up for myself and what I wanted and needed. Becoming friends with him was familiar and since we had a long physical distance between us, I wanted what was familiar."

"Monique, how were things when you two became friends again?"

"Well, I was guarded, but it was his personality that broke me down. He was funny and I love a man that can make me laugh. He was my friend and he was back in my life; life was good. During this time, I started seeing someone. While my body was with someone else, my mind and my heart were with Ronnie. My being with someone else was my way of getting back at him for disappearing. Plus, he never wanted to make a commitment to me. In his eyes, we were just friends and I felt that at the moment there was no way I was going to change that. So with that, I sought physical love and attention elsewhere."

"So, if I am hearing you correctly, you are saying that you let him back in because you were lonely and missed his friendship? Is that a fair statement, Monique?" asked Dr. Shores.

"Yes, I guess so," Monique said with the shrug of her shoulders. "I loved that man. I felt that if he was going to come back to me, I was going to take him back."

"Did you ever tell him that you were seeing someone else?"

"No, not initially, but he figured it out."

"How did you feel about it when he found out?"

"Honestly?" Monique asked.

"Yes."

"I felt vindicated and sexy. I felt like it was a big Fuck You to him. To me, that symbolized me saying, 'you didn't want me, so I found someone who did."

"How was your relationship with him after he found out?"

"It didn't appear that anything changed. I felt that he knew where we stood—that we were just friends, even though I wanted more. Had he told me he wanted to be with me, I would have gladly stopped seeing the other guy."

"Monique, have you thought about how your mother's relationships with men have affected your own relationships?"

"No. Since my last visit, I've tried to put it out of my mind. I see where you are going, and that is a subject that I am just not ready to deal with yet."

"Okay, I can appreciate your acknowledgement that it's a subject that you aren't ready to delve into. However, you may want to address these underlining issues before your child is born."

Monique didn't comment. She sat in silence and looked off into the distance. Folding her arms, she thought that Dr. Shores was probably right. But she couldn't take another deep and emotional moment.

Dr. Shores spoke up, "Let's tackle your request to 'move on.' Perhaps we should also discuss your previous relationship. That could be the cause of you not getting over this one. In my practice, I have noticed that women tend to take baggage with them. Baggage that you have picked up, good or bad, from a previous relationship and put them in your hobo or satchel bag and brought them with you to your new relationship."

Monique looked at her with a puzzled look.

"You said that your break up with your ex hurt you deeply, right? Did you tell Ronnie about your ex and how he hurt you?"

"Yes, I did. What does that have to do with anything?" she asked.

"When you told him, did you expect him not to do those things because another guy did them to you and, subsequently, hurt you?"

Shrugging, she said, "I guess so."

"You put expectations on him because of all the dirty laundry your ex had deposited in your shoulder bag. Our goal while you're here is for us to buy a new empty purse. You will wear it proudly. There will be no dirty laundry from your last relationship. You will only collect positive items that make up who Monique Daniels truly is. When we interact with others and build relationships, we learn things about ourselves in the process. Those are the items that I want you to store in your new bag. For instance, Monique doesn't like white wine. She tried it with Steve and realized it's not for her. That little notation makes you Monique Daniels. Not, he left me and I can't get over it. Understand?"

"I hear what you're saying, but I don't know how to do that. The 'dirty laundry,' as you put it, is who I am now. This is me," Monique said, putting her hand on her chest.

"We are not defined by our circumstances or our dirty laundry. And for the record, dirty laundry can be laundered. If you feel that is what makes you, then we will take all your laundry to the cleaners. My goal is to give you a new 'empty' bag. You will get through this and come out on the other side with a new bag."

"If you say so. Right now, I need to focus on today. I have a baby coming and I am not with its father."

"We'll take it one week at a time, Monique. Have you told the father that he has a child on the way?"

"No, I haven't. I am barely accepting it myself. The only people that know are you, my best friend, and Dr. Johnson. I haven't even told my mom."

"I understand. Do you think that the father will benefit from sharing in this experience with you?"

"I'm sure he will, however, I don't really know anything about him. We met at a bar, and I went back to his place and we had sex. It was a one-night stand. I was feeling very vulnerable and lonely and I decided to have sex with him. He gave me his contact information in case I needed another 'release' as he called it, but I never called him. When I was in college, I vowed to myself that I would not have a one-night stand ever again. The last time that happened, I ended up getting gonorrhea. I'm not ready to tell the father or anyone else right now. I told my best friend about the baby and she's so ecstatic that I had to get off the phone with her. I couldn't stand all of the congratulations and questions about the father."

Monique noticed that Dr. Shores had a questionable look on her face. She tried to clean it up, but failed. Monique didn't hold it against Dr. Shores; we're all human.

"Based on what I know about you, you'll get there. It is just going to take some time. How far along are you?"

"I am a little over a month pregnant." Monique began to fidget. She wanted nothing more than to get out Dr. Shores' office. The subject was causing her to be uncomfortable and she didn't want to discuss her situation anymore today. She looked at her watch which read that her time was up.

"Monique, are you ready to leave?"

"Yes, I need to get out of here."

"That's no problem. We can pick up next week." She stood up to shake Monique's hand. "Have a great week, Monique. Live in this present moment, not in the past."

"I've got no choice, Doc." Monique left Dr. Shores' office.

Chapter 6

After being holed up at home thinking about her last session with Dr. Shores, Monique was ready to get out for a while. It was Thursday and her date with Mason was that afternoon. Monique called Lena to ask her for fashion advice, but was unsuccessful as Lena was a little grouchy when she answered. Monique decided to make her selection on her own.

While sifting through her closet, Monique narrowed her choice down to two outfits: a purple peplum dress that she could wear with cute wedges or a black sheer, silk blouse paired with a red pencil skirt with an exposed zipper. She decided that she would be *killing 'em* in the red skirt. This would definitely be her choice for the day. She got dressed and gave herself a once over in the mirror before heading out the door. Monique had to admit she looked pretty good.

Lena called Monique on her way to work. "Okay, so what did you decide to wear?"

"I picked that outfit that I wore to the play that we attended a few weeks ago."

"Cute, I am sure that you will look nice on your *non-date*."

"Non-date is right. We are just hanging out after work. And before you say it, I just wanted to look cute. It's nothing major."

"Whatever! I'm about to walk into work, I'll call you later to see how your *non-date* went. Bye."

"Bye girl, have a good day."

When she got to the office, Craig was already there. They exchanged pleasantries and started to work on their project. Monique thought about telling Craig that she was pregnant. He would be happy for her but knowing Craig, he would have so many questions and she wasn't ready to answer anyone's questions yet. Interrupting her thoughts was the buzz of her cell phone.

Mason: HAPPY THURSDAY MONIQUE. I HOPE YOU HAVE A GREAT DAY AT WORK.

Monique: HI MASON, HAPPY THURSDAY TO YOU TOO. HERE'S WISHING YOU A GREAT DAY AS WELL.

Mason: I AM LOOKING FORWARD TO SEEING YOU AND HANGING OUT WITH YOU TONIGHT.

Craig caught Monique smiling at her phone "What, or shall I say who, is making you smile like that?"

Monique put her phone down. Smile now gone. She hadn't realized that she was smiling. She really shouldn't be smiling because Mason was just a friend. Nothing has happened, *yet*. "Hush, it's just a text from a friend."

"Some friend. I haven't seen you smile like that in a while. Whoever he is, enjoy it."

"Funny you should say that. This guy is a just a friend, truly. We are getting together tonight to catch up on old times."

"If you say so. All I'm saying is have fun. There is no reason to rush into anything."

Monique gave him a puzzled look regarding that comment. She wasn't sure where it was coming from. Perhaps, he was talking about his own marriage. All she could muster was "I got that covered." She decided she needed to downplay this little outing tonight with Mason, although she was bubbly on the inside about it. It was now that she realized why Lena didn't want to say anything about her conversation with Mason. Who knows what the future holds with Mason. She didn't want to get her hopes up, or his.

Monique: I AM LOOKING FORWARD TO HANGING OUT TONIGHT WITH A GREAT FRIEND.

There, that should do it. Now he knows this would be nothing but two friends getting together.

The project that Monique and Craig had been assigned was in Iowa. Monique had never been to Iowa, but she was up for the challenge. The hospital wanted to build a children's hospital to add to its portfolio of services and hired the firm to design the addition. Getting out of Clover would be good for her.

Monique's plan was to leave work a little early so she could get to Charlie's Place before Mason. She wanted to hide out in her car before he got there so she could check him out before going into the restaurant. Unfortunately, a last minute meeting called by Mr. Patterson, the firm's owner, appeared on her calendar. If this meeting took longer than five minutes, she was going to be late.

She tried to keep her mind on the project that she and Craig were working on, but her mind kept wandering to the meeting with Mr. Patterson and her non-date with Mason. Luckily, Craig had an appointment so they concluded their work on the project early that day. Monique was thankful for the break. She needed the opportunity to clear her head before her meeting with Patterson. When she walked into the conference room, Mr. Patterson was in the room with Leo and they were in a deep conversation about football.

"Hi, guys," Monique said shyly when she walked into the conference room.

The two stopped talking and turned to look at her.

Mr. Patterson greeted her. "Thanks for coming in at the last minute. I will make this quick. You've been with the firm nearly seven years now, is that correct?"

"Yes, I have," she answered hesitantly. She didn't know where the conversation was going. She skipped out early last Friday, but so did everyone else. Perhaps they were going to give her a new assignment, she thought.

"Well, as you know from the meeting last week, Leo will be stepping down from his position soon. I wanted to be the first to tell you that you are on a short list of candidates that we are looking at to take on the role as interim managing partner."

Monique was shocked, and it was written on her face—mouth open and eyes bulging. She did tell Craig she was interested, but she hadn't thought anyone would really consider her for partner. *Close your mouth, Monique.*

Leo spoke up. "Yes, Monique, you've done great things at this firm and we've taken notice. Many of your projects come in under budget, leaving the client happy with the end result. I am stepping down to start my own firm as it has been a dream of mine for years."

"That's wonderful," Monique said. "Congratulations, Leo. Thank you both for considering me for the role. I am definitely interested in the position."

"We will make our decision next week," said Mr. Patterson.

"I appreciate you letting me know. Thank you," Monique said as she got up to shake their hands.

"Before you go, Monique... Please keep this confidential. We wouldn't want word spreading before we make our decision."

"Yes sir, and thanks again." Monique walked out of the conference room elated. If she was selected for the position it would definitely propel her career trajectory. She knew that she shouldn't have, but couldn't help herself. Craig was in the office when she got back so she told Craig everything. He was so happy for her and her potential future at the firm. "This is wonderful news, Monique! Want to grab a quick drink and celebrate?"

Monique was about to say yes when she checked her watch. So caught up in the excitement, she totally forgot about her dinner with Mason. She was supposed to be at the restaurant in fifteen minutes and with rush-hour traffic starting, there was no way that she was going to be on time. "Rain check?" she asked Craig. "I am supposed to meet that friend I was telling you about for dinner at 5:30 and I am already running late."

"Of course," he said, hugging her. "I'm so happy for you. Let's celebrate when it's official," he said smiling at her. "You are good at your job and would be a great managing partner."

"Thank you, Craig," Monique said as she was grabbing her purse. "I've got to go."

"Enjoy yourself, Monique," Craig said with a wink.

In the blink of an eye Monique was on to the next thing, her non-date with Mason. She wondered what they would talk about and if it would be awkward, now that she knew he had been asking about her. Feeling herself getting nervous, she called Lena from the car. "Lena, I am on my way to meet Mason. What are we supposed to talk about?"

"What do you mean what are you supposed to talk about? He's your *friend*, right? Talk about things that you've always talked about. Now I really wish I wouldn't have told you that he was interested."

"Oh, don't say that. I'm glad that you told me so that I could be prepared. Our relationship hasn't been the same since we all went on the trip, so it may be awkward. Give me some topics that we can discuss. Should I tell him about the baby?"

"I don't know. That's up to you. If he's your friend, you should tell him. You can also talk about work or address *whatever* happened during the Dominican trip that you don't want to tell me about. Talk about why you wanted to change your date from lunch to dinner."

"Shut up, it's not a date. I sure as hell don't want to bring up the trip to you or him. If I don't tell him about the baby, I'll have to make up something about why I'm not drinking."

"Whatever, you'll tell me about the trip one day. How far away are you?"

"I've got about another fifteen minutes to go. Good thing he texted me to let me know that he was running late. How was your day, Lena?"

"Wait, are you actually asking me about *my* day? I am shocked."

"Why you say that?"

"While I love you, all of our conversations have been about you lately."

"Have they?" Monique asked. "I didn't realize, I apologize." Monique was upset to hear that she had become the needy friend. Swallowing her guilt, she repeated, "So how was your day?"

"It was actually pretty good. I was able to get plenty of writing done. I am ready for this process to be over, but a writer's job is never done. There is always another book to write. How was your day?"

"It was great, actually. I found out that I am on a short list for interim managing partner at the firm. Don't tell anyone."

"Really? That's awesome. Congratulations! Who am I going to tell? I don't know anyone that you work with. Is being interim something that you want?"

"Yes. I think I would be good at that position. And who knows? It may turn into something permanent. Finally, something positive in my life."

"Well good luck. I hope you get it. And good luck with your *non-date* with Mason. I can't wait to hear all about it. Be good."

"Thanks. Bye, girl."

Monique never thought of herself as someone that would monopolize a conversation. She prided herself on being that person that her friends and others could depend on. And now she was the needy one. This situation with Ronnie and the pregnancy had changed her. She didn't like being the person that needed other people, but that was what she had become. That little comment from Lena had taken her mind off of her "date" with Mason.

She and Mason arrived at the restaurant at the same time. Mason was of medium build, about 5' 9. His dimples were eye catching, and his light brown eyes added to his model physique. He was very attractive and had a smile that lit up a room. His sense of humor kept those in his presence in stiches. A healthcare consultant, he was always getting promoted and made plenty of money for his firm. While he was both successful and attractive, he hadn't been in a relationship longer than six or eight months—a serial dater. He could always attract women, but he was never satisfied with his selections. He once told Monique that something was missing with every woman that he dated.

They parked next to each other and once they got out, they gave each other a hug. It was awkward for Monique knowing that he had been asking about her. She didn't know how to respond. When they walked into the restaurant, Mason led her to the bar and waved the bartender over to take their drink orders. Monique ordered cranberry juice with a splash of lime and Mason ordered a Heineken. He frowned at her drink order, but didn't speak on it. Monique saw the question register on his face about her drink order. She was grateful when he didn't speak on it because she definitely wasn't ready to divulge that she had a little one on the way. She decided to break the ice, "To what do I owe the pleasure of your company this evening? You said we needed to catch up. What's going on, brother?"

"You get right to it, don't you?" he asked. Their drinks arrived just in time. They both quickly grabbed them and took a few sips to distract from the awkwardness. "Well,

Monique, I wanted to see you. We haven't talked in a while. How are you?"

"You wanted to see me? Why?"

"Because who wouldn't want to see a beautiful woman? We haven't hung out since the Dominican trip. I missed you."

Monique almost choked. "You missed me?"

He didn't answer her question. Instead, he repeated his original question. "You didn't answer me the first time, so I'll ask you again. How are you?"

"I'm well, not much going on personally," she said with her eyes downcast. It was too early to talk about all that was going on with her. She just wanted to celebrate the fact that she was out of the house and hanging out for a change. She changed the subject, "How was your day?"

"Actually it was pretty good. It's even better now that I'm out with you. Hey, there is a booth over there that's open," he said pointing. "Let's move over there."

Monique noticed that the booth was a little secluded and a little more private than the bar. Mason picked up their drinks and the two moved to the booth. Once they were seated, Monique spoke up, "Oh wait, I do have some news. I am being considered as interim managing partner at the firm."

"Hey, that's exciting. Congratulations! We'll have to celebrate when you get that position. I'm confident that you will. You're good at what you do."

"Thanks, Mason. I am excited about the opportunity. It will be just the step in the right direction that I need to propel my career."

"Shall we order some food? It's all on me tonight."

"Whoa, that's nice of you. One might say that this was a *date*."

"I hope that you do."

Monique looked directly at Mason, "where is all this coming from?" She had to ask.

"Okay, I have been waiting on the right moment for the past year to tell you that I am interested in you. I asked Lena if you were still seeing Ronnie and she told me that y'all were over, and had been over for a while now. And I asked you out tonight so that I can tell you that I want to date you."

Monique had no words. When she started talking to Ronnie, she stopped hanging out with Mason as much. He would call and ask her to hang out but she often declined. And then the Dominican trip happened. "I had no idea. What brought this on?"

"I have just kept my feelings at bay since I knew you were dating the other guy. I didn't want to overstep. And now seems like the right time."

"What about our friendship? What if we start dating and realize that we were better as friends?"

"We would go back to being friends."

"Sorry, Mason, but I doubt very seriously that we would be able to go back to being friends, especially when sex is involved."

Mason was in mid-sip when she mentioned sex. He choked on his drink. Setting his glass down he said, "Monique, we can take it slow. I would like for us to date."

"Is this something that I can think about? There are few things going on in my life right now, some things that I need to take care of. "

"Absolutely, I don't mean to rush you. My goal was to make you aware of how I felt."

Monique blushed. She couldn't believe that Mason was so blunt about his feelings for her, nor could she believe that she jumped from a few dates to sex. They had a lot of mutual friends and seeing him at various functions may be awkward if it didn't work out. However, dating Mason would help to propel her in getting over her ex-friend. *But how would he feel about the little one?*

Changing the subject, Monique updated Mason on some of their friends. They also caught up on each other's family and discussed their career aspirations over dinner. Throughout their conversation, Monique couldn't help but to think that he *really* liked her. She bit her lip at the thought. In her mind, she jumped from having a friendship with him to him helping her take care of the little one. From walking down the aisle to wondering what their children would like. She hated that her mind wandered like that. It happened every time a guy expressed an interest in her. She would fantasize about marriage before she even knew the guy. She made a note to bring this up in therapy.

After he paid the bill, the two got ready to say their goodbyes when that awkward moment of *do we kiss or don't we* showed up. Monique fumbled with her coat and purse. Mason just stood there waiting for her. He knew his friend well. He knew that she was nervous about ending the evening and waited for her to stop fumbling.

"Monique, I had a great time tonight," he said as he grabbed her hands. "I hope that we can continue to have more evenings like this." He took her hand in his and led her outside to their cars. Monique had no idea where he was going with his statement. When they got outside to her car, he added, "I will leave the ball in your court, if we take this further or not. However, I will continue to pursue you. If you decide that a friendship is all that you want, then I'm okay with that. I just want to be in your life." He leaned in and kissed her on the cheek and allowed his lips to linger there.

Monique tried not to show any outward emotion, but on the inside she was hot. She let go of his hand, and gave him a big hug and held him around his neck, reaching up on her tippy toes. She whispered in his ear, "Goodnight, Mason." He stood there and waited for her to get in her car before heading to his.

A real gentleman.

• *Chapter 7* •

When Monique woke up, it was as if something was awakened in her. She was refreshed and renewed. Mason taking her out to dinner was the jolt she needed to see the world differently. For so long, she had been living in the past as the victim and she had been carrying around the hurt of the things that had been done to her. After her date with Mason, she decided that life is for the living and that she needed to live for the future of her little one and not in the past. Monique determined that today she was going to have a good day at work. She had a session with Dr. Shores later that afternoon, and thought it'd be good to bring her new school of thought with her.

When Monique got to work, she was offered the interim managing partner role. She gladly accepted and told the partners that she would do them proud and uphold the company's mission in every way she could. She was to start her new duties the following week. She would shadow Leo for two weeks, then move into his office after his last day.

Craig and a few other coworkers treated Monique to lunch to celebrate. They were all very happy for her and her success. Finally, there was something positive in her life that she could celebrate. After they returned to the office, Monique called her mother to tell her the good news. Her mother was very delighted and told her that she would send her something special in the mail. When their conversation hit that moment of lull, Monique's mother told her about her new boyfriend Roger. It seemed to Monique that her mother was more excited about Roger than she was about her promotion. After a few sessions with Dr. Shores, Monique could see that her mother's happiness was in fact based upon being with a man. Monique abruptly got off the phone with her mother. She couldn't stand the fact that Dr. Shores was right. She needed to finish up her day and head to her session with Dr. Shores.

Driving to her appointment, Monique reflected on the day's events. She'd woke up that morning determined that she was no longer going to be the victim.

She concluded that it was her date with Mason that made her wake up to the fact that she no longer wanted to live in the past. Why didn't she have the resolve within herself to wake up to that notion? Why is it that an interaction with a man had to awaken that in her? Why didn't she have the tenacity to do it on her own? She made another mental note for therapy discussion. The mental notes were piling up.

Monique started as soon as she walked into Dr. Shores' office. "Dr. Shores, I have to tell you that I was very agitated the last time I was in your office. I think everything just hit me all at once—past, present and future. I have been reflecting on your comments regarding baggage, and yes, I think that I do have baggage and dirty laundry. It affected my relationship with Ronnie and quite possibly the relationship with my child's father. Here's what I need to do: I need to get to a point where I can get the dirty laundry cleaned and taken out of my bag. I woke up this morning refreshed and ready to start seeing the world as the victor and not the victim."

"Okay. But may I ask what brought this on?"

"I had a date with a friend last night and it opened my eyes to the fact that I have been living in the past and that life is happening now and it's time that I start living in the now."

"I understand. Let's go back. How do you think your baggage has affected you?" Dr. Shores asked.

"Well, I mentioned that the break up with my ex-boyfriend affected this 'friendship' with Ronnie."

"Wait, I need to sit on the chaise..." Monique grabbed her messenger bag and got up from the couch and moved to the chaise. Monique sat back, looked at the ceiling and continued talking, "This relationship was about ten years ago. We dated for about a year and half. While we were together, I found out that he was married. He didn't tell me he was married. He failed to mention it. We lived in two different cities and had a long distance relationship. During our relationship, he was a reservist and was sent to Iraq. And now that I say that out loud, I don't know if even that was true. He was truly a con-artist. He came out for a visit one weekend, and I saw a piece of mail in his things addressed to a woman that shared his last name and address. I asked him about it and he told me I was being ghetto.

I put him out of my house and my life that weekend. As soon as he left, I started doing research, which is something I should have done from the start. I found his marriage license online. He got married six months before we met. Later, when I fully confronted him about it, he said he got married for insurance reasons, as his wife was a reservist as well. I eventually got over it. The baggage from this relationship is probably why I always prefer that people be upfront with me and tell me the truth. I guess that's why it hurt so much when Ronnie just disappeared the first time and ended things the last time. I can't answer why I accepted this behavior from Ronnie. Perhaps it was because he was around and no one else was showing interest in me at the time. It wasn't until I got ready to go on vacation to the Dominican Republic that I learned the true reason as to why he cut off communication."

"Okay, so why did he end things?" asked Dr. Shores.

"It all starts at the airport, on my way to the Dominican. I was sitting in the Hartsfield-Jackson Airport in Atlanta waiting on my connecting flight. I just so happened to look up from my game of Words With Friends to see a pretty little girl around one-year old. She was playing with her toys, sitting on her mom's lap. They were waiting at the next gate on their way to San Antonio, TX. I told the mother that her daughter was very cute. She said, 'Chelsea, tell the nice lady thank you.' Chelsea waved to me with her toy in her hand. The mother struck up a conversation with me, saying that she and her fiancé, Chelsea's father, were going to San Antonio to get married that weekend on the River Walk. I congratulated her. She went on to say that Chelsea's dad went to get them some lunch, as their flight had been delayed for a few hours due to the bad weather in San Antonio. Since they had three hours to kill, they would have to entertain Chelsea and hope that she tired out for the flight.

"I went on to tell Chelsea's mother that my biological clock was ticking and that I was at that stage in my life where I was ready for children. I told her that with every child I see, I long for one of my own. She told me that Chelsea was a surprise to them, but that she was a gift from God and that they cherished the day that they were blessed with her. As we continued talking, the gate agent for my flight announced that my flight had been delayed for two hours. 'Oh, that's just great,' I said. 'Now I'm going to miss my welcome reception with my friends when I arrive.' I told Chelsea's mom that I should go find some lunch for myself since I was going to be there for a while.

"The entire time she and I were talking, I felt someone watching me. I looked around, but saw no one. It isn't until I got up to leave that I looked up and thought I saw Ronnie. *Nah, that's not him. Can't be.* It wasn't him, thank God. I told little Chelsea that I would return. She waved at me again but with a different toy in hand.

"About forty-five minutes later, I return and see Chelsea and her mother still sitting there. This time, their positions changed and they looked like they'd eaten. Her mother told me that I missed her future husband. She said he had to take a phone call but would be back at any moment. She asked if I was dating anyone and I told her no, that I just got out of a rough relationship and dating wasn't on the horizon for me at that moment. She gave me her card and said that there is something about me that she really liked. She told me that she was a matchmaker with a 100% success rate. She told me that she would like for me to give her a call after my vacation and asked how I was going to get that bun in the oven without a mate. Then she commenced to tell me how she and her fiancé met. Their story sounded like one of true romance. She went after him first. Once she had his attention, the tables turned and he pursued her. Chelsea was the result of too much wine; her words not mine. They were finally making it official. Then she asked, 'Where is Ronnie? I would really like for you to meet him?'"

"At the mention of his name, I felt my bowels move in the pit of my stomach. When I felt someone watching me, it was Ronnie. This was his fiancée and his child. I had been drawn to them, and they were about to get married! Ronnie walked up with his head hanging low. 'Amanda, I see you have met Monique.' Amanda gasped, 'You are Monique?'

'Hi, Amanda, it's very nice to meet you.' Though that's what I said, it's definitely not what I was thinking. *Why would God do this to me today? Why would I encounter them on my way out of town? I just had to meet Ronnie's fiancée and child as they are on their way to get married? Really?* What was God trying to teach me? I prayed right there, 'Dear Lord. I am going to need your help in trying to forget this one so I can have a good vacation. Amen.'

"Dr. Shores, I sat up there and told this woman that my biological clock was ticking and she had the nerve to give me her card and say that she wanted to fix me up with somebody. She stole my man and pretty much told me how she did it. Ronnie then said, 'Monique, I am glad that you were able to meet my family. I am sure that Amanda has told you that we are on our way to get married.' With his hands stuffed in his jeans pockets, he went on, 'I never meant for you to find out this way, but I'm glad it's all out in the open. I wish that we could remain friends.'" The emotions of that moment washed over me all over again.

"I was dumbfounded and had no response. In my mind, I was thinking, you've got to be kidding me. Why would I be your friend? I am still hurt over our relationship-slash-friendship. Just as he was about to go into detail, the gate agent for my flight announced that we could leave earlier than initially thought. I thought God must have my back. I told them that it was a very awkward and chance meeting. I congratulated them and wished them the best, and told them that my flight was getting ready to leave. As I was packing up my carryon luggage, Amanda—feeling guilty for stealing my man—says, 'Monique, my offer still stands. I really am a matchmaker. When you get home from your vacation, give me a call, seriously. I would love to match you up.' I told her that I'd think about it. The gate agent announced that my flight was boarding. 'That's me. Chelsea, you take care of your parents.' She looked up at me and actually waved with her hand that time. I walked to my gate and never looked back."

After explaining the airport encounter, Monique sat back on the chaise and closed her eyes.

"Wow! That is some story. Did that chance encounter affect your trip?"

"Yes and no."

"Explain."

"When I got to Punta Cana, I was very vulnerable and wide open." Monique paused and reflected on the events that happened in the Dominican. "Dr. Shores, I am not ready to discuss what happened in Punta Cana. I almost lost a very dear friend due to my actions on that trip."

"Okay. Let's go back a step and explore the relationship with your ex."

"What do you want to know?" Monique asked, looking over at Dr. Shores.

"Did he end things, or did you choose to?"

"Really, Doc? I ended it. How could I stay with him while he was married?" *Even though I did just text Ronnie and I know that he is definitely married. Good thing he didn't respond.*

"If he were upfront and told you the truth, would you have stayed in the relationship?"

Monique looked at Dr. Shores as if she had horns growing out of her face. "No, I don't share. But it's funny that you should ask. This man still calls me today, ten years later as if nothing happened. He was an older guy and, throughout the relationship, I felt as if I needed to be reverent to him. You know, give your elders respect. While we were together, he had a surgical procedure that required a hospital stay. He didn't give me his room number and I didn't think anything of it. I figured that he didn't think I would visit because I lived out of town. I felt that it was perhaps an oversight. I got to the hospital, approached the front desk and asked for his room. The volunteer at the desk asked me for my identification. I questioned why she needed it. She told me that he had a list of approved people that were allowed to visit. And do you know what? My name was not on the list. I left the hospital and never told him about it. I just used that as an opportunity to find out what I was dealing with. That incident should have been my first clue that he was no good."

"Monique, it sounds like you always end up blaming yourself. However, it appears that you aren't placing the blame where it should be, which is on these men. Perhaps you were a little naïve, but these men don't deserve your empathy. They were wrong. I see why you have dirty laundry. You can't let what they've done to you define you."

"I don't know...I did allow it to happen."

"Okay, so you were jaded and couldn't see past it. However, these things were done to you. Next week, let's explore your trip and the things that transpired after your meeting with Ronnie at the airport. Throughout the week, I want you to reflect on how that interaction at the airport affected you and your trip."

"Okay, Dr. Shores. There you go... the past will be visiting me again and trust me, it won't be in the office."

• Chapter 8 •

As Monique was walking out of Dr. Shores' office, she called Lena. "Lena, how do you know Dr. Shores again?"

"Well, hello to you too. How did your session go?"

"She gets me every time. By the end of the session, I walk out of there either crying or mad. She has me bringing up all these old thoughts and feelings—feelings I didn't even know existed."

"Well, it sounds like it will help in the long run. She is likely trying to get you to revisit those old feelings to get to the root of your issues with men."

"Issues with men? Where did you get that I had issues with men?"

"Monique, I am just calling it like I see it. You end up in one bad relationship after another, and now you are stuck on one that ended over a year ago. Am I right?"

"Yes, you *are* right. I guess I just never thought I'd hear my best friend tell me that I have issues with men. It kind of hurts."

"It was not my intent to hurt you. I'm just being real."

"So, how did you come to know about Dr. Shores?"

"Oh, it was no big deal. She helped me work out some issues I had in the past."

"You had issues? I don't believe it. You are the most together sister I know."

"Let's not get into it. She helped me and I'm cured. End of story."

"If you say so. Guess what? I was named the interim managing partner today. The bosses called me in the office to ask if I wanted the position and I accepted. We need to celebrate. Hold on a minute." Monique's phone buzzed in her ear.

678-555-3470: HELLO MONIQUE. HOW ARE YOU?

Monique felt a rush from her head to her toes. A number appeared on her phone that was all too familiar. Although she had deleted his number from her phone, she still knew it by heart. It can't be. I don't believe it. "Uh, Lena, why did he just text me?"

"He, who?"

"He equals Ronnie."

"What? What does he want?"

"I don't know. Should I respond?"

"No, let that son of a bitch *alone*. Don't give him the respect of responding to his text. Let me tell you something, just because a man texts you does not mean that you owe them a response. You don't owe him anything."

"Calm down, Lena. Don't get all feministic on me now. If I text him, what should I say?"

"I don't know, Monique. Why would you waste your time talking to him?"

Smiling, Monique said, "I'm curious as to why he's reaching out." It was the thought that Ronnie was thinking about her that pleased her most. She felt as if she was his toy and now he had pulled her off the shelf to play with her. But he was married and had ended their friendship with a text message. He didn't even have the decency to tell her that he had a child, or that he was seeing someone while they were 'friends.'

"Monique, you do you. I am in no position to judge you. When he breaks your heart again, know that I'll be here to help. I've got to go. I'll talk to you later." Lena hung up before Monique could say bye.

She couldn't understand why Lena was so upset. There was something that Lena wasn't telling her and she needed to find out why Lena needed Dr. Shores' services. Monique decided to text Ronnie back. What was the harm? She'd just make her response blunt.

Monique: WHAT?

Her phone buzzed.

678-555-3470: I MISS YOU.

Monique: LAST TIME I CHECKED FACEBOOK, YOU WERE HAPPILY MARRIED.

678-555-3470: YOU'RE RIGHT, I AM. I JUST MISS YOU. CAN WE TALK?

His response pissed her off. How could he be happily married and yet text her that he missed her? Monique contended that he's a jerk and that her life was much better without him. At this point, Monique decided to take Lena's advice and not respond. She didn't need him. His text asking her to talk scared her so much that she turned her phone off. She made up in her mind that she was not going to let him ruin her evening.

Hours after Monique got home, she turned her cell phone back on. She had a few texts from Lena and Mason. Mason's text asked for another date which reminded her that she needed to tell him about the little one. No need in stringing him along and not telling everything that was going on with her. Lena's text wanted to know how things went with Ronnie. She knew that Monique had texted him back. As she was responding to Lena, her phone rang.

"Hello?"

It was Lena. "What he say?"

"Girl, I was just about to text you. He asked me if we could talk. He said he missed me. What the hell is that about?"

"How did you respond?"

"I didn't. I turned my phone off. I am just now turning it back on."

"Are you going to talk to him?"

"I don't know. What do you think?"

"I think you will. Sending you that text is just what he needed to reel you back in. He laid the bait and you took it. Now, I am not coming down on you. You're a grown woman. You do what you want to do. It's just that I have been in a situation similar to yours, and I don't want to see you make the same mistakes I made. It was hard for me to get back to being myself, and I don't want that for you. You deserve better."

"Is that why you were a patient of Dr. Shores?"

"No."

"So, why were you her patient?"

"Monique, I never said I was her patient."

"Yeah, you did."

"No, I said she helped me work out some issues. I didn't say that I was her patient. Can we just leave it at that?"

"Lena, what's the big secret?"

"There isn't a secret. I just don't want to talk about it. It's in the past. Let's just leave it there."

"Whatever."

"I didn't get a chance to tell you congratulations on your promotion earlier. I am so proud of you. I knew you could do it. When do you officially start in your new role?"

"I start on Monday. I am thrilled about it! This opportunity will give me more experience that I can add to my resume."

"Don't overdo it, Monique. You have a lot of things going on in your life: new role, new baby and Mason—all while you're trying to get over Ronnie. Not to mention that he is trying to worm his way back into your life."

"I get it, Lena. Okay. I get it. I will take it easy. Enough about my day, how was yours?"

"Actually, my day was pretty good. I finished up some copyediting for a client. I received a bonus for turning it in early. So that's two new pairs of shoes for me."

"How about you save that money?"

"Nah, I am going to spend it. No need to save it. Let tomorrow worry about itself."

Monique cocked her head to the side in a quizzical manner. Dr. Shores had used the same phrase in one of their sessions. Why would Lena choose the very same phrasing if she wasn't a patient? She decided to let it go for now.

"By the way, Mason asked for a second date. I want to see him again. This time, I will go ahead and tell him about the little one."

"Good for you. I like the two of you together as a couple. I don't know what it is about him, but I like him for you. You never really told me about the first *non-date*."

"Well, actually I asked him if that was a date and he said yes. Girl, he said that he has been feeling me for a while, and that he was just waiting on the proper time to step to me. I was not expecting that, especially after the trip to Dominican. That was such an embarrassing time for me. I was very vulnerable and wide-open from seeing Ronnie and Amanda in the airport. I am supposed to discuss it in my next therapy session."

"Boy, I sure wish I could sit on that session to get all the juicy details."

Not addressing her comment, Monique went on, "on another note, I picked up a book about what I should expect in the next eight months and I want to read tonight to prepare for my little one."

"Have a good night. Before I let you go, I want to apologize for coming down so hard on you earlier. I just don't like to see my friends hurt. Be careful. That's all I can I tell you."

"Thanks, Lena. I appreciate you saying that, and I accept your apology. Good night, friend."

"Night."

Her phone buzzed.

Mason: I HOPE I WASN'T TOO FORWARD AT OUR FIRST DATE. I MEAN OUTING...

Monique: NO MASON, YOU WEREN'T. YOU BEAT ME TEXTING YOU BACK. YES, I WOULD BE HAPPY TO GO OUT ON A SECOND DATE WITH YOU.

Mason: AWESOME. SHALL WE GO TO THE NEW BISTRO ON 11TH FOR LUNCH ON SUNDAY?

Monique: OH THAT WOULD BE GREAT. I'VE BEEN WANTING TO GO THERE.

Mason: SEE YOU THEN. HAVE A GOOD NIGHT BEAUTIFUL.

Monique: GOOD NIGHT.

Monique took out her journal. She decided to write instead of read.

Dear Lord, thank you so much for this incredible gift that you have blessed me with, a child. I never thought I would be in this place, unwed and knocked up. However, I am trying to find the silver lining in it. I will have my very own child, someone for me to love unconditionally and someone to love me. God, I don't know how I am going to do it alone. I know I should tell the father, but I am just not ready to go back down that road. God, I don't want him involved with my baby. Yes, I said it...my baby. You have given me the blessed gift O God and I don't want to share my little one. I need you God.

• *Chapter 9* •

A week had passed and it was time for Monique's weekly session with Dr. Shores. This week, she had a mid-morning appointment as opposed to an afternoon appointment as she had videoconferences for work every afternoon that week. Although she was promoted, she was still carrying the workload from her previous role. Before promoting her, the company neglected to tell her that she would still be responsible for her current projects. "Morning, Dr. Shores," Monique said as she entered the office. Today, she opted to sit directly across from Dr. Shores and not on the chaise lounge. "How are you doing today?"

"Hello, Monique. You seem to be glowing today. I am fine, thank you for asking. How are you today?"

"Actually, I feel pretty good. I don't think I mentioned in the last session that I was promoted at work. Right now I am training with my predecessor. Once he leaves, I will be the interim managing partner at the firm. I am very excited about the opportunity. I also have another date with a friend in a couple of days, and I have come to accept my little one."

"Congratulations on the promotion. That is great news. Is this something that you want?"

"Yes, it is. I have always wanted to move up in the company."

"I am very happy for you. Let's go back to this date with a friend. Is this the same friend that you mentioned in our last session?"

"Yes, it is. Sounds weird, doesn't it? Mason and I have been friends for a while and he just expressed his feelings for me. He told me that he had been interested in dating me."

"How do you feel about him?" asked Dr. Shores.

"I'm having fun with Mason."

"Are you interested in him? Or are you using him to fill a void left by Ronnie?"

"Damn, Dr. Shores, really? Why can't you just be happy for me?"

"Monique, I am happy for you. I am just asking what your level of interest is in your friend. What happens if things don't work out?"

"I don't know. I asked him the same thing. If it doesn't work out, he said that we could go back to being friends, but I disagree considering that a line would be crossed. To answer your question, he's definitely someone that I could get into. He's a gentleman and I know that he would treat me well."

"Are you attracted to him?"

"Yes, he is very handsome. We have a good time together when we hangout. I like him. I guess I never looked at him as more than a friend until now. In fact, when we hung out recently, I was imagining what our kids would look like. Is that crazy?"

"No, that's not crazy. We women always tend to desire the next thing, hardly enjoying the moment. Have you told him about the baby?"

"I haven't told him yet. I am a little worried that it would ruin whatever it is we are trying to start."

"When are you planning on telling him?"

"This weekend. We made plans to have lunch on Sunday." Monique's phone buzzed. It was Ronnie. She resaved his number to her phone.

Ronnie: I AM REACHING OUT TO YOU AGAIN, SINCE YOU DIDN'T RESPOND TO MY TEXT. CAN WE TALK?

Monique read the text, and threw the phone back into her purse.

"Something wrong?"

"No. I apologize for even reading the text during our session."

"It's your dime, not mine."

"I see you have a sense of humor," Monique commented with a raised eyebrow.

"Are you ready to discuss what happened on your trip, after you ran into Ronnie, Amanda, and Chelsea?"

"I guess so." Monique shrugged not really wanting to discuss the trip. She had tried her best to put it out of her mind. She sat back and crossed her legs.

"I am ready whenever you are."

"Well, when I walked away from them and boarded my flight, I tried my best to display confidence. I held my head up high and marched right onto the plane as to say kiss my ass. *Take y'all's sorry asses and go to San Antonio, of all places.* But on the inside, I was crushed. Yes, I was about to go spend a week in the Caribbean, but I had been deflated by the news that he was getting married and that he had a child. It hurt more than anything to know that he left me to be with his child's mother. I was let down that he had stopped communicating with me, but it hurt more that he left me for someone else. When I got on the plane, I prayed and cried. I cried because I was hurting; I prayed for strength and happiness. I prayed that God would spare me the hurt feelings and usher me into bliss during my vacation. It didn't work. Well, let's just say He didn't come when I called....

"When I arrived at the hotel, I had to wear my sunglasses—not because of the sun, but because my eyes were puffy and red from crying. I tried my best to hide it on the plane, but failed. The flight attendant, an older sista, noticed me crying. She came over to me and actually sat with me, as there was no one else on my row. Apparently, she saw the whole thing unfold at the gate. She gave me tissue and words of encouragement. She told me that God had a better plan for my life and that soon this incident would be a thing of the past. Her kindness made me cry even more. She sat there with me and held my hand for most of the flight, when she wasn't serving the other passengers.

"That was probably the most heartfelt love that I had ever received from a stranger. It touched me. That humanness of her reaching out to me in my time of need made me very grateful. She told me that he didn't deserve me and that everything would be okay. That God was going to take care of me. When I got off the plane, I wanted to thank her, but I couldn't find her. It was as if she just disappeared. I looked for her at the gate, in the nearby restroom, at baggage claim, but she was gone. I'd like to think that she was my very own angel.

"Shortly after I arrived at the hotel, all of my friends did too as their flights were delayed as well. By the time they found me, I was on my sixth drink at the bar at the all-inclusive resort. I didn't tell anyone what happened. As far as they knew, Ronnie and I were over and had been over for quite some time. Not feeling like talking, I left my friends and went to the beach. It was there in the sun that I passed out. I was awakened by a familiar face—Mason. Apparently, he had been watching me and looking out for me since I left them at the bar. When he approached me, he had so much loving concern in his eyes that I started to cry all over again. Half of me was drunk, and the other half was still hurting from what Ronnie and Amanda had revealed to me at the airport. He left me to get tissue. By the time he returned, I was a snotty mess.

"He really tried to console me. I didn't tell him anything about what happened at the airport; I didn't want anyone to know. He figured out that I was crying over a guy. He was rubbing my back while telling me that everything was going to be okay. That calmed me down. It calmed me down so much so that I mistook his kindness and gentleness as him flirting. And since he was flirting with me, I decided to return his gesture with more flirting. I kissed him in mid-sentence as he telling me that everything was going be fine. He kissed me back. We continued to kiss. I received his passion and gave him my pain. Before I knew it, we had walked back to his room. His roommates were with mine at the bar. There was no one to catch us in the act. We got to his room and I undressed him. I was still fully clothed. When I reached his pants, I unzipped them. I got on my knees. I was ready to drink watermelon. My mouth was on him. A minute into it, we heard our friends outside the door. I ran in the bathroom. He zipped his pants. I sobered up quickly when I saw myself in the bathroom mirror.

"I didn't recognize myself. My eyes were swollen and red. My hair was wild from being windblown. I had sat outside so long that I was tanned with raccoon eyes. It was not attractive and I could not believe that I seduced a friend like that. I walked out of the bathroom and our friends urged us to come to dinner. I made up some excuse to leave. I couldn't look Mason in the eye. I tried my best to avoid him the remainder of the trip. On the last night, he asked me to go for a walk with him on the beach. Hesitantly, I accepted. He told me that he noticed that I had been avoiding him. He apologized for letting our actions get out of hand. He said that he shouldn't have allowed things to get wild and that his flesh got the best of him. He said that he only meant to comfort me. He told me that he was shocked that I kissed him and was willing to do other things to him. I tried to stop him from talking because I didn't want to talk about it. I was so embarrassed and ashamed of my actions that just talking about it made me cringe. I thanked him for being a friend and for caring about me. I laughingly told him that I never wanted to talk about our incident, nor hear about it from anyone else. He nodded and gave me a hug. He said our incident would go with him to his grave. I thanked Mason for his friendship and we continued walking in silence. When we caught up with our friends, and he and I were back to being "normal" as if nothing had happened. I was only playing the part. I was still a little uneasy about everything. I have never told anyone this story, not even my best friend."

"How do you feel now that you told me?"

"I feel better. It's bad, but not as bad as I have been making it seem in my mind. I hate that seeing that little family prior to my departure had me drunk and ready to have sex and ruin a friendship."

"How was the trip outside of your incident with Mason?"

"It was actually pretty good. Once I had a good night's sleep, I was okay by the next afternoon. Seeing them had an effect on me, but it wasn't as bad as I had anticipated. Prayer changes things. I prayed that God not let that incident ruin my trip and, for the most part, it didn't. He was right on time."

"So how has your relationship with Mason been since that meeting?"

"We've talked on the phone a few times, but we really haven't seen each other since then, until we went out a few weeks ago."

Dr. Shores removed her glasses and crossed her legs. She looked up at Monique. "Did you two discuss what happened on your trip when you saw him?"

"No, it didn't come up. And I don't really want to discuss it with him again. It happened, we moved on."

"So why do you think you two haven't talked or hung out since then?"

"Good question. I guess I was avoiding him, but honestly, I am over it. I just don't like talking about it."

"And yet, you were avoiding him?"

"Can we move on?"

"Monique, are you okay? You're grimacing."

"No, I am not. My stomach is hurting. I guess this a part of having a baby, right?"

"Yes and no. We are almost finished here if you want to contact your physician."

"Okay."

"Is there anything else you want to discuss before your session ends?"

Monique sighed. She hated that she was so transparent. "Yes, Ronnie texted me. He wants us to talk."

"How do you feel about that?"

"I don't know. With everything that has gone on, I shouldn't even respond to his text. However, I want to know why a happily married man would want to reach out to me?"

"What is your plan?" Dr. Shores asked.

"I think I am going to see what he wants. I am a curious person, and at times this gets me into more trouble than not. Speaking of being curious, I was referred to you by my friend Lena Booker. When I asked her how she knew about you, she didn't go into detail. Are you two friends?"

"Why the curiosity, Monique?"

"I have really benefited from our sessions, and I was just surprised that Lena has someone like you in her toolbox."

"It's nothing really. No fascinating story."

Monique knew that she was not going to get anything out of Dr. Shores, so she left it alone. Looking at her watch and standing, Dr. Shores extended her hand to Monique—a sign that her session was over. "Monique, next week, let's discuss the outcome, if any, of you and Ronnie connecting." Shaking her hand, Monique agreed and told Dr. Shores that she would see her next week.

"Okay, thank you. I hope everything is okay."

"I am sure it will be. I will see you next week," Monique said.

• *Chapter 10* •

Monique felt better once she left Dr. Shore's office. The cramping had stopped and she decided to text Ronnie back. What did she have to lose?

YES, WE CAN TALK. WHAT TIME?

He responded immediately – I AM IN CLOVER CITY. LET'S MEET AT WAYNE'S PLAZA AT 11:45A.M. THEY HAVE A FEW PRIVATE AREAS WHERE WE CAN TALK WITHOUT INTERRUPTION.

Checking her watch, she saw that it was 11:00. She only had 45 minutes to mentally prepare seeing him again.

OKAY. I WILL SEE YOU THEN.

Monique was allowing herself to take the passenger seat on this roller coaster, yet again. Instead of her taking charge and telling him where and when she could meet, she allowed him to tell her. She drove to Wayne's Plaza and sat in the parking lot. She wasn't ready to go in. She needed to have a pep talk with herself first. *Okay, see what he wants. Don't show any emotion. Be emotionless, Monique. If you find yourself slipping and falling for bullshit, catch yourself and get up. Dust yourself off by remembering all that he has done to you. You can do this.*

In the midst of her pep talk, she saw him pull up in her peripheral. She used this opportunity to go inside before he had a chance to see her. When she walked in, the hostess asked how many. In times like this, she was happy to say two instead of one.

"Can you seat us in one of your private areas?"

"All of the private areas are taken right now. We have a semi-secluded table for two. Would you like that or would you prefer to wait?"

"I will take the semi-secluded. My guest is coming in soon. Can you go ahead and seat me? I don't want to wait."

"My pleasure. Please follow me." The waitress seated Monique and soon returned with Ronnie. He came over and greeted Monique. He kissed her on the cheek and the forehead. *Damn him.*

"Monique," he said. "Thank you for seeing me. You look really good. You're glowing."

"Thanks, Ronnie. You don't look bad yourself." Monique had to admit, he looked good. She could tell that he had put on some weight, but it looked good on him. When he came over to greet her, she smelled Creed. That scent always did something to her. Ronnie was 6'1 with a large build. He carried himself as if he if knew he looked good, but that was what had attracted Monique to him in the first place, in addition to his good looks. He had beautiful smile that made Monique melt every time she saw it. On top of that, he wore glasses, which perfectly complemented his look.

"Thank you for meeting me. I know this can't be easy for you," Ronnie said.

She stared at his wedding ring. It was two-toned with white and yellow gold and had a few diamond baguettes, shining as if to say, *"Hey, look at me. I'm married!"* He noticed her staring and he moved his hand to his lap.

"What do we need to discuss, Ronnie?"

"You haven't changed. I can tell that you're nervous and are trying to be calculating. You don't have to be that way with me."

Monique bit her lip and looked away. He had always known her. He knew her moves before she made them. "Since you know me so well, get on with it."

"I don't know how to tell you this, but I am still in love with you. Seeing you at the airport confirmed it for me. I have been torn with what to do, if I should tell you or not. Something told me that I should try to reach out, especially since you texted me the other day. I felt that if you chose to respond to my text, then you would be open to hearing what I have to say. I have love for my wife, I do, but I am still in love with you. I have never stopped loving you. I know you're probably wondering why I would marry her if I were in love with you. It's because I didn't want to hurt her. She and I already had Chelsea, and it seemed like the logical next step." Ronnie stopped talking. He must have read the shock and disgust on Monique's face.

"I don't believe you."

"Believe it. I know that doesn't make me sound like the greatest guy, but it's the truth. I felt that you needed to know the truth. Amanda and I hooked up once and she got pregnant. I wanted to do right by my child."

"Here is the truth, Ronnie. I have been in therapy because of the shit you did to me. You cut me off without so much as a clue as to why. We weren't a couple, so when I asked you if you were cutting off my friendship, you said yes. What the hell was...?" She felt her temperature and her blood pressure rising. She needed to calm down. She lowered her voice. "What was I supposed to do with that? Why are you here anyway? In the two years that we were friends, you never thought it was important to come out here, so why are you here now?"

"I know I did a number on you. I've been in therapy too. My therapist told me that I have unresolved love. Sure I am married, but I married for the wrong reasons. Amanda and I got married so we could provide a good home for Chelsea. What am I doing here? Well, Amanda got a promotion at work and we moved here for her job about four months ago. We live about an hour out of the city." Grabbing Monique's hand, he said, "I miss you baby."

The touch of his hand sent shockwaves through her body. Softly she asked, "What am I supposed to do with that?"

Ronnie rubbed her skin. "I don't know what you are supposed to do with it. I just needed to tell you. Amanda and I aren't doing so good. She knows the stronghold that you have on me. She almost turned the job down because it meant that we would need to move here. She hates that we are so close to you." Ronnie pulled his chair closer to hers so that they were sitting side by side. He started rubbing her back and asked, "Are you okay? You are so beautiful to me." He kissed her cheek then began kissing her neck. He knew that was her spot. Monique turned her face to him and just stared at him. He kissed her. She kissed him back. He rubbed her thigh. Sliding his hand away from her thigh, Monique said, "I can't do this. You hurt me. You broke my heart, not once but twice."

"I know and I am sorry," he said as he began to nibble on the nape of her neck.

Monique let out a small moan. She was about to kiss him back when a woman appeared at their table. Monique sat straight up. Without looking up, Ronnie said, "We're not ready to order just yet."

"I knew you would do this. I knew just as soon as we moved here, you would meet up with her. And now, my worst fears have become true, you're cheating on me."

Ronnie jumped at the sound of his wife's voice. "Amanda, it's not what it seems."

"It's exactly what it seems. It looks like you are having an affair with Monique."

Monique grabbed her stomach. It started cramping again. She did not want to get involved in this dispute; she was the innocent one.

"No, I meant our marriage is not what it seems. I am in love with Monique. We only got married for Chelsea, and you know it."

"Oh no!" Monique got up from the table, clutched her hobo bag and ran to the restroom. When she reached the stall, her fears were confirmed: She had been spotting and was in a lot a pain. As she peed, blood and clots began filling the commode. Her mind told her that she was losing the baby. She reached in her bag and took out her cell phone and called Lena, "Hello….Lena…I'm losing the baby. I'm in the restroom at Wayne's Plaza, can you come get me?"

"Yes, I am right around the corner from there," Lena said. "I'll will be there in ten minutes. I'll call Dr. Johnson too."

"Okay. See you soon," Monique moaned.

The door to the restroom opened and it was Amanda. "So what does the home wrecker have to say for herself?" she yelled.

Guttural sounds were coming from the stall where Monique was.

"You two have been planning this the whole time, haven't you? What am I supposed to do, Monique? You think you're just going to take my man without a fight? No way. I am not letting him go that easy. Having him in our lives means the world to Chelsea, and I am not going to deprive her of a father. That's why I selected him in the first place. When I found out I was pregnant, I decided that he was going to be the father. So don't think that just because we moved here that he is going to leave me that easily."

The only response from Monique were whimpers.

Amanda continued. "What's wrong with you? Do you hear me talking to you?"

Monique couldn't respond. The pain was overwhelming. Hearing Amanda rant about Ronnie only added to her pain. Minutes later, Monique heard the door to the restroom open.

"Monique, where are you sweetheart?" asked Lena.

"Down in the handicapped stall."

Lena asked, "Are you still bleeding?"

Amanda gasped at what she heard and grabbed her chest, "Oh, no."

"No, it's stopped, but there's a lot of blood."

"That's okay, go ahead and flush," Lena told her. "Come on out and I will take you to the emergency room. Dr. Johnson said that we should go there so they can confirm if you've had a miscarriage."

Monique came out of the restroom, crying. "Oh my God, Lena. I can't believe that I lost the baby. I didn't even get a chance to tell the father."

"It will be okay." Lena wrapped her arms around Monique's waist and helped her friend out of the restroom. Lena looked at Amanda with disgust because she stood there staring at them still holding her chest. When they got in the car, Monique started, "Why God? Why would you do this to me? I know I was slow to come around in accepting my little one, but I loved it and you took it from me."

"Everything is going to be okay," Lena said, patting Monique's leg.

When they reached the emergency room, the ER doctors performed an ultrasound and doctors confirmed Monique's suspicions—she had miscarried. Monique wept silently as the doctors told her that she could expect more bleeding and cramping over the next couple of days. It was all a blur to her.

After it was all over, Lena took her home, had her shower and get in bed. Monique was a wreck. In a catatonic state, she did whatever Lena told her. Once she got in the bed and was off to sleep, Lena went to her house to get a few things so she could stay with Monique for a few days. Monique slept for about twenty minutes before her phone buzzed. Mason had texted her.

ARE YOU OKAY? LENA JUST TOLD ME WHAT HAPPENED. WHAT CAN I DO?

Thanks Lena. Monique called Mr. Peterson to tell him that she would need be off for a week. She needed to clear her head. When she told him that she miscarried, he gladly obliged her. After her phone call, she drifted back off to sleep. In her dream state, she remembered all the events of the day. Ronnie told her that he still loved her and Amanda had confessed to her that Chelsea wasn't Ronnie's child. She was awakened again by another text message.

MONIQUE, I HOPE YOU'RE OKAY. AMANDA TOLD ME THAT YOU MIGHT HAVE HAD A MISCARRIAGE. I'M HERE FOR YOU – ANYTHING YOU NEED. LOVE YOU, RONNIE.

Throughout the night, Lena tiptoed in Monique's room to check on her. She was awake every time Lena opened the door. Whenever she was able to doze off, she was awakened by the memories of what happened that day. She decided to get up and write in her journal.

Today, I lost the love of my life—my little one. I don't even know if it was a boy or girl. There is nothing like losing a child. Even though I didn't know him or her very long, I loved my little one. As I look around my room, I have bags of all types: small, hobo, satchels, body bags, backpacks and all others in between. I have a lot of baggage, literally and figuratively.

Dr. Shores said that I needed to start getting rid of my baggage. It was probably the stress and the heaviness of my bags with all of its dirty laundry that caused me to lose my little one. Of all things, Ronnie professed his love for me today. He kissed me and I kissed him back. I can't believe that I allowed that to happen. Would I really get back with him now that that Chelsea isn't his child? So much drama!

But then again, I have more baggage, Mason. He is a great guy, a real gentlemen and a good friend. He wants more, but honestly, it would be a rebound thing. I would feel safe with him, but I know my heart is still with Ronnie. God, please help me to get rid of the baggage. I can't do it without your help. You are all-knowing, and you know what is best for me.

Please help me through this loss and help me to lose the baggage. I guess my loss is the cost of baggage. Take it all away from me God, clean house.

Amen.

• *Chapter 11* •

After a few days of Lena being at her house, Monique sent her home. She had been a godsend. She had taken her to doctors' appointments, cleaned and cooked dinner for her, but Monique really needed to be alone with her thoughts. She assured Lena that she would be okay. She filled Lena in on all the drama that preceded her miscarriage. Needless to say, Lena was shocked to find out that was Ronnie's wife was the woman in the restroom with them. The pair laughed at Amanda and how she was spilling her dirty laundry in the restroom of all places. Mason, Ronnie and Craig had been texting her to see if she was okay. Intermittently, she texted Mason and Craig to let them know that she was well. She would have to get her mind right before she responded to Ronnie.

Monique called Dr. Shores' office. She needed to see her. While her appointment wasn't for a few days, she felt that she needed to speak with her today. Dr. Shores' receptionist, Courtney, was able to squeeze her in later that afternoon. In the past week, Monique's life had been turned upside down. The loss of her child made her want to get things in order, finally. She had to stop living in the past and focus on her present and future. Monique arrived at Dr. Shores' office a half hour early because she had nothing else to do. Walking into the office, she heard a familiar voice in the waiting room. It was Lena talking to Dr. Shores. "Rainy, you crazy, girl. I've got to get out of here. Tell Mama Carolyn I will stop by later to see her."

Monique was shocked to see the two so familiar. "Lena? What's going on?"

"Oh goodness, Monique. I didn't expect to see you here."

"So you two are friends?"

"Yes, we are Monique," Dr. Shores responded. "Lena and I were roommates in college."

"We had some wild times back then," said Lena. "We lost touch for a few years, but we reconnected via Facebook."

Monique folded her arms, "Finally, you tell me. What was the big secret about that? You could have told me that when I asked you. Wait a minute, is this the reason why you wouldn't answer your phone a few weeks ago?"

"Yes, it was fun to watch you squirm with curiosity. I didn't want to distort your view of Lorraine and the professional service that she would provide to you. Rainey and I got into a lot of trouble back then. She helped out more times than I can count. I will have to tell you about it one day," said Lena.

"Lena, you can't taint my patients with my dirty laundry. Go on get out of here. I'll tell Mom you said hello."

The two embraced, then Lena turned to Monique, "I suggested Rainey because I knew she would help you reach your full potential. I will call and check on you later." Lena hugged Monique before leaving.

"Monique, come on in," said Dr. Shores. "What brings you in today?"

"Lena didn't tell you?"

"No. Lena wouldn't betray your trust like that. We keep things like this totally separate."

"Okay," Monique said not fully believing her. She shoved her hands in the pockets of her hooded sweatshirt.

"Are you uncomfortable knowing that Lena and I are friends? Would you like for me to refer you to another therapist?"

"I don't know. I saw the way you two interacted, and I want to be a part of that. It's odd. No, let's just keep it the way it is. I will just have to rationalize that you are my therapist and not my friend. But that you and my best friend are friends... weird."

"Okay. If you feel uncomfortable at any time, I can always refer you. So, what brings you in today?"

"Well, Dr. Shores, in the last few days, so much has changed. Before I get into that, I need to tell you that I am really ready to get rid of my baggage. Baggage has done nothing but cost me. How do I get rid of the dirty laundry?"

"We will take it one step at time. You've been slowly coming to this conclusion over the last couple of sessions. I will give you some homework and things to think about, and essentially you will do the work. I will just coach you along. Tell me what brought this epiphany on?"

"I had a miscarriage, for one. When I sat down and really evaluated the things in my life, I believe that I had too much going on. I had an STD, was stuck on Ronnie and trying to get something started with Mason, a promotion at work and I neglected myself and my child."

"Monique, I am sorry to hear about the miscarriage. Do you think it started with the cramps you were having in my office?"

"Yes, I miscarried later that evening. I am doing okay with it, but I definitely feel the loss. I am taking it a day at a time." Monique went on to detail the other events that day with Ronnie and Amanda.

"Where did you leave things with Ronnie and his wife?" Dr. Shores asked.

"I haven't. I know I have to, and I will likely take care of that today, but I wanted to come see you first. I need to start on the path of cleaning up my dirty laundry and getting a new empty bag."

"I am glad to hear that. After all that has happened with Ronnie and his wife, how do you feel about him now?"

"I have resolved that I have to take care of me first. There is a part of me that will always love Ronnie, but right now, I have to do me. It's a shame that it took a miscarriage to wake me up to that. I get sick thinking of all the time I wasted stuck in the *he hurt me* phase. There is so much more to life. While he professed his love, and I appreciate him being honest with me, there are certainly things that he is going to have to work through and I cannot be a part of that. I will not *allow* myself to be a part of that.

"If I can step back in the past for a minute, I can acknowledge that he hurt me—and that hurt was real. I honestly don't know if him professing his love for me is enough to forgive him. And right now, he has other issues. He just found out that the reason he claims he got married isn't even true. That is definitely too much drama for me. And then there is Mason, who has been such a sweetheart, calling to check on me every day. Right now, I don't know if I have it in me to date him. I will have to tell him that he will have to settle for my friendship. But it does help to know that he is interested." She smiled.

"Monique, I am proud of the progress you've made."

"Thank you. I can't say that I won't slip up and have some regression. Like I said, I am taking it a day at a time. Losing my little one was a wake up for sure."

"Some regression is expected. We are all on journey to be better tomorrow than we were yesterday. Here," she said, handing her a very nice leather bound journal. "I know that you journal, but since you are ridding yourself of baggage, start fresh with a new journal. Remember, when you journal, make sure you are writing about both the good and the bad. It is important to have good days and bad days chronicled when you look back on your past and reflect. This will also help you to answer the question of what make Monique happy."

"This is really nice. Thank you. Yeah, I think I am going to need some time to answer that question."

"You have asked me for my help with getting you on the right path, but you have started that journey all on your own. You should be proud of yourself. Before we move on, did you ever tell the child's father about the baby?"

"No, I didn't. I resolved not to tell him. I figure not telling him is best. What he doesn't know won't hurt him."

"Okay, as long as you have come to a resolution about it. When we meet next week, I want you to come back with actionable steps that you can take if you feel yourself stepping back into your closet to pull out an old bag."

She laughed. "Now, that is funny, Dr. Shores. I will work to come up with a list. Thank so much for squeezing me in today. I appreciate it. And I don't need the number for another therapist. I would like to continue being your patient."

• *Chapter 12* •

It was the last day Monique had off before returning to work. She used the week to clear her head after the miscarriage and all of the drama. She had to clean up and the bags had to go. Someone would be happy to receive them. Monique received a call from Ronnie. She decided that now would be the perfect time to address the situation with him.

"Monique," he said. "Are you okay? I have been worried about you since we met at the restaurant."

"Yes, I am okay. I had a lot going on and was not able to get back with you. I received all of your text messages and thank you for your concern. I did have a miscarriage. However, I'm taking things a day at a time."

"I am so glad to hear that you are doing okay. I understand that Amanda blurted out to you that Chelsea is not my daughter."

"Yes, she did."

"She ended up telling me all about it, afraid that you were going to use it to get back with me. I have been going through it. I love that little girl as if she is my own. Amanda and I have separated. We are taking the court-ordered steps required for divorce. I cannot believe that she tricked me the way she did. I sure could use your help, friend."

"Ronnie, I can't. I will not allow myself to take on that type of drama, especially when I don't have to. A part of me will always love you, but I love myself much more. I have to take care of myself before I take care of anyone else."

"Wow, who is this new Monique? There used to be a time when I could tell you I needed you and you would always try to help me figure things out."

"Times have changed. I wish you the best. Maybe when you get yourself together, we can talk."

"I will look forward to that day. I would rather have you in my life as a friend than not at all. Too much time has gone by without you. I miss you and our friendship. I love you, Monique. Have a good day."

"Bye, Ronnie."

Monique went to work on plans for her new closet. She had researched various storage options and had designed a closet that she would work out for her. She would add a built-in shelving unit for the bags that she decided to keep and for her shoes. Now all she had to do was start cleaning. The phone rang again, this time it was Mason. She was rather popular that day. "Hi, Mason."

"Hey, you sound as if you are in good spirits."

"I am. What's up?"

"Well, I want to take you out to lunch today. Can I do that?" he asked.

"Yes, I will gladly go with you to lunch, but only as friends. I don't think my life can take any more than that right now."

"That is not a problem for me. I cherish our friendship. I will be there to pick you up at 11:45 a.m."

"Okay, I will see you then."

Monique hung up the phone and went back to her closet. She didn't need to call Lena to ask her what she needed to wear. She was going to lunch with a friend and any outfit she picked would be fine. Mason arrived promptly at 11:45 a.m. When Monique opened the door, Mason was standing there with yellow tulips, her favorite.

"Mason," she said. "Thank you for the flowers. Come on in."

"You're welcome. I thought it would bring some cheer to your day."

"That is very thoughtful of you, thank you. Shall we go? I want pizza."

"Pizza sounds good. Let's go."

At lunch, Monique told Mason about her plans to do a little spring cleaning. She didn't go into detail as to why. She only told him that she needed to clean out her closet. He told her that he would be happy to help. Monique tried her best to tell him that he didn't have to do it, but he insisted. When Mason dropped Monique off at home, he walked her to the door. "Thanks for agreeing to have lunch with me. I really needed to get out of the office and see a friendly face."

"Well, Mason, I am glad that I could be there for you, just as you have been here for me throughout all of this mess. I appreciate your friendship."

"So do I, Monique. I will see you tomorrow." The two hugged and Mason left to go back to work.

Monique really appreciated his friendship. He didn't constantly ask her how she was feeling about losing the baby. He seemed to only want to be there for her, which is what she needed in her life.

<h1 style="text-align:center">• Chapter 13 •</h1>

oday is D-day. I have to clean out my closet and am working on cleaning up my life. God, in the wake of tragedy, you have helped me. You have opened my eyes so I can truly see the blessings that I have. I have great friends that support me. I have an awesome career with a new position, and I now have a better sense of who I am. Getting to know who I am has been the greatest blessing of my life. Today will be a great day. Thank you for always being in my corner.

Monique's doorbell rang at 10 a.m. It was Mason and Lena there to help her with spring cleaning. "Hi guys," Monique said. "Come on in. Are you all ready to get started? Let me warn you: I haven't cleaned like this since I have been in this house."

"What? You are buying lunch, right?" asked Lena.

"Of course. Whatever you guys want is on me. I'll even spring for adult beverages. I am sure that will make the conversation lively."

"I can't believe that I am about to clean with two women. The fellas will never let me live this down," Mason said.

"No one ever has to know," Monique said with a wink.

"Well, I definitely won't tell them," Mason said, smiling back at Monique.

"Excuse me, what are the looks and innuendos about?"

"Nothing," Monique and Mason said in unison.

"Whatever."

"Okay, let's get started. Mason, can you start by putting all those bags in the Dress for Success bin? Those bags have weighed me down for quite some time now. I am sure that there are plenty of women out there that can benefit from having them."

The End